THE BROKEN PIECES OF US

Matt and Rosie's Story

Celia Tandy

**Copyright©2023 Celia Tandy
All rights reserved.**

ISBN-13: 9798858694212

Dedication

To Mark and Liya with my love

KINTSUGI – joining with gold

In Japan, they sometimes repair broken pottery with gold. The flaw is seen as a unique piece of the object's history which adds to its beauty.

Kintsugi is also a metaphor for life. Through acceptance and resilience (and in this story, love) we can heal and become stronger – imperfect yet still beautiful.

PROLOGUE

The antique grandfather clock chimes the midnight hour, its jarring sound breaking the sombre silence in the house. Every fibre of my body strains as my ears pick up the soft creaking sound of Jackson's bedroom door opening, and then his slow, methodical footsteps ascending the stairs. They stop abruptly outside my bedroom door, and then I hear his wheezy breathiness and his urgent tap, tapping against my door.

"Rosie, let me in," Jackson whispers gruffly.

I sit frozen, staring at the inside of my door, my whole body tensing and on high alert. My heart races wildly, my ears filling with its loud drumming noise as if it's determined to escape my body.

"Don't play hard to get," Jackson whines, his voice becoming more raspy and angry. "Come on darlin', open the door."

He pushes heavily against the frame, but the chair I've jammed against it holds firm. I wait, silently praying that he'll give up now and go back to his room. "You want to play games, huh? You may not have me in your bed tonight, but I promise you will, you little slut."

I shudder at his hard voice, and my veins compact with fear like razor sharp icicles invading my body. He's drunk, and I'm scared he'll wake his wife if he gets any louder but, after what seems forever, his heavy footsteps slowly return downstairs. I breathe out shakily, gasping for air that I seem to have held in, my head throbbing with a dull ache. This is the third night in a row, and I'm petrified of Jackson and what he might do to me.

Over the last month, I've tried so hard to make this job a success. I'm a companion and carer to Jackson's wife, who has Parkinson's disease. She's a sweet woman and I look after her while Jackson works in his study, but every day he leers at me and makes up excuses to get me alone. I'm constantly dodging his unwanted advances, and I'm appalled that he's being so blatant in front of his sick wife.

I pull down my worn suitcase from the top of the wardrobe and quickly throw in my few clothes and possessions. Then I sit rigidly on the edge of my bed, waiting. The old mahogany clock continues to tick rhythmically over the next hour, while I stare at my bedroom door, waiting for Jackson to fall asleep.

After I've exhausted my patience, I carefully pull the chair away from its position and turn the doorknob slowly to open it. It creaks loudly, the sound deafening in the stagnant quiet of the slumbering house. My body tenses with fear, but I risk creeping out a little way onto the landing. The moon casts eerie shadows through the half-open curtains, and I wonder if Jackson's lying in wait. The thought terrifies me.

As soundlessly as I can, I carry my battered suitcase downstairs to the hallway and warily make my way past Jackson's room to the front door. My hands shake uncontrollably as I fumble to unlock the heavy bolted door, and a sob escapes me in frustration. Eventually, the door clicks open, and I run to my car, throwing my suitcase into the boot, just as I see a light turn on in Jackson's room.

I drive away into the darkness, tears trailing silently down my cheeks. Once again, I'm alone without a home or job and, worse, no one in the world to care.

Chapter 1 – Rosie

What the hell was I thinking, drawing my prospective boss on a pantomime horse?

I'm late, I'm late! For a very important date! The words from the White Rabbit in Alice in Wonderland echo in my head, and an exasperated sigh leaves my lips. A jack-knifed lorry and two frustrating hours sitting in a massive tailback on the M5, and now I'm late for my job interview. It would be a great job too, but my chances of getting it are slipping away like grains of sand through an hourglass. Still, I guess I've nothing to lose by showing up and hoping my prospective employer will forgive my delay.

I find the Equestrian Centre easily enough on the outskirts of a pretty Cotswold stone village and, as I drive slowly up the gravel driveway, I take in its beautiful countryside setting. There are majestic oak trees in the distance, and the soft late afternoon sun lights up the verdant fields on either side of the drive. There are several chestnut and dapple-grey horses standing lazily in a large paddock to my left, and what looks like some stable blocks and a riding school beyond.

The driveway curves around, past the Equestrian Centre, and finishes outside the front of an attractive two-storey house. The house is large, honey-stoned, and appears to have been substantially extended from the original building. There's a magnificent flowering wisteria, like a mauve waterfall, cascading over the front of the older part of the house, and the side addition is modern but still in keeping with the original features.

Taking a quick glance in the car mirror, I comb through my hair, spritz perfume and apply lip-gloss. What am I doing? Mr O'Connell won't care if I'm wearing lip-gloss or not. In fact, I'm so late, he'll probably order me to turn around and send me packing. I take a deep, calming breath and knock on the front door more confidently than I feel inside.

After a moment, a man wearing dark denim jeans and a black T-shirt opens the door. He has a tea towel draped over his shoulder, and he stares down at me with a confused frown on his face. "I'm Rosie Anderson, Mr O'Connell–"

But before I can say anything further, he snaps at me, "You're late!"

He's in his early 30's, tall with thick dark brown hair which curls slightly into his neck and a five-o'clock shadow, which adds to his overall grumpy look. His lips pinch together in a tight line of disapproval, and I hold my breath, waiting for the inevitability of his rejection.

We stare at each other for a long moment, neither of us saying anything, and then my eyes wander downwards, taking in his taut chest beneath his tee. I may have briefly lost concentration because he suddenly clears his throat. I drag my eyes upwards again where they land on his dark, moody eyes, which are looking at me with bemusement.

A kaleidoscope of butterflies takes flight in my stomach, and my cheeks heat under the intensity of his stare. "Yes, I know. I'm so sorry. There was a big holdup on the motorway, and I got stuck in the most enormous traffic jam. I would have rung, but my mobile's out of charge. I got here as soon as I could…" My voice trails off.

I'm suddenly aware of another voice shouting in the background. The voice sounds urgent. "Dad…. Dad… I can smell burning. Daaaad…."

Mr O'Connell (a.k.a Mr Moody) seems distracted by whatever's going on inside the house and frowns at me in frustration before moving to one side, inviting me in. He strides ahead and I follow, looking curiously about me. The hallway has various pairs of children's shoes and trainers abandoned on the tiled flooring, and tossed carelessly by the front door is a school bag.

We enter a large open-plan kitchen, and sitting at a farmhouse-style table in the centre of the room is a young boy surrounded by paper and coloured pencils. I already know that Mr Moody is a widower, and this must be his son, because he has the same mahogany eyes as his father, although his hair is much lighter. I smile at the little boy because he's the reason I'm here, and it's vital that he likes me if I'm to stand any chance of becoming his new nanny.

"Damn," Mr Moody curses, as he throws burnt toast into the bin and puts more into the toaster. "You'd better sit down while I finish making supper. This is Tobias." He looks towards the child.

He turns his back on me and begins frying sausages. The smell is lip-smacking delicious and my mouth waters. For some inexplicable reason, a wave of contentment sweeps over me. It's as if I've finally found my rightful place in this kitchen with the small boy and the tall, moody man. I shake my head at how absurd I'm being and try to focus on why I'm here.

"Hello, Tobias, I'm Rosie."

The boy's eyebrows draw together in a deep furrow, and he glares at his father. "My name's Toby NOT Tobias."

"Ah, okay. I'll always call you Toby." I give him my best reassuring smile.

Glancing down at the paper in front of him, I see that he's drawn a picture of a dog with brown and white fur, a bit like a Border Collie. I wonder if they own a dog, but I can't see any sign of one. Then Toby suddenly looks at me and says dramatically, "I want a dog so much my tummy hurts, but dad says I can't have one until I'm older."

Deciding it's not a good idea to get involved in an argument between father and son on what's plainly a sensitive issue, I hastily change the subject.

"Can I have a go?" I ask, and he hands me a blank sheet of paper. I select a coloured pencil and begin sketching a larger-than-life pantomime horse, with a moody looking man sitting on top wearing an oversized Stetson.

"That's my dad!" Toby bursts out laughing, and I glance sideways at his father, hoping I haven't annoyed him further, but thankfully he's ignoring us. I pick up another coloured pencil and this time I sketch Toby with a monkey sitting on his shoulder. I make the drawing as funny as I can, giving the monkey exaggerated features and a wide cheeky smile.

"That's a picture of me." He grins in delight at my drawing.

Luckily, I was always good at art at school, and maybe my silly sketches will make Toby like me even if his dad's still giving me the cold shoulder. After a moment, he chooses another pencil and begins sketching a girl who looks like me, holding a fat orange cat with enormous saucer shaped eyes.

"Look, Rosie!" He points at the drawing excitedly.

"That's brilliant, I love it! What will you draw next?"

"Umm…Belle on a horse." I've no idea who that is, but I nod encouragingly.

Toby giggles and starts on the picture while I warily observe his father's profile. I heave down a sigh. Even his back looks irritated. Still, it's nice that Toby's making me feel welcome, even if his father's blatantly ignoring me. A minute later, Mr Moody finally turns around.

"Your tea's ready, buddy. Please wash your hands."

Toby jumps down from his chair and stands on a small children's step by the Belfast kitchen sink to clean up. Meanwhile, I gather up his drawings and move a table mat into the space so that his father can put down the plate of food. There are scrambled eggs, buttered toast and two perfectly golden-brown sausages on the plate. My stomach growls with hunger. I haven't eaten anything all day, and I'm starving.

Mr Moody must notice me drooling over the food because he finally looks at me, his face questioning. "Would you like some toast and coffee?"

"Thanks, that would be lovely." My stomach rumbles loudly again. I actually hate coffee, but I don't want to risk appearing rude, since he appears to be thawing a bit towards me.

Toby returns to the table, and while he's eating, I take in my surroundings. A large oak dresser sits along one side of the room, and there are a couple of comfortable wingback chairs and a sofa next to an unlit wood burner. Several drawings, presumably Toby's, are stuck onto an American-style fridge. And, allowing maximum light into the room, floor-to-ceiling sliding glass doors take up the whole of one wall and lead to an outside patio area and a garden beyond. It's contemporary, tasteful and the ambiance, in contrast to Mr Moody, is cheerful and relaxed.

Toby's father places two slices of toast in front of me and hands me a covered butter dish so I can help myself. I surreptitiously try to take in more of his appearance. His eyes are still stormy, and his angular jaw's set with a frown. His body is muscular and strong like he's used to heavy physical work, and his voice has a deep, rumbly tone that sounds commanding and sexy. *What am I saying? Commanding and sexy!* Stop it, I tell myself off sternly, but the mob of butterflies is back, leaping about in my tummy.

Finally, he sits down at the table with a mug of coffee, his eyes inscrutable as he studies my sketches. *What the hell was I thinking drawing my prospective boss on a pantomime horse when I'm desperate to get this job?*

"So, you want to work as my son's nanny, but I see from your C.V that you don't have any relevant experience?" His eyes move from the sketches to my face.

"I haven't got any nanny experience, but I have some experience in a caring role. My mum was ill for a long time, and I took care of her." It sounds lame, but I press on. "My last job was looking after a lady with Parkinson's. I know I haven't got any childcare experience, but I really want this job, and I'll do my best to be a kind and caring nanny to your son."

Tears prick the back of my eyes. What's the point? I'm not qualified at all for this position, and he could easily find a more experienced nanny to look after his son. I've no idea why the agency even forwarded my C.V.

His dark, intelligent eyes study me, and I steel myself for his rejection, but then Toby breaks the silence. "Rosie, will you teach me how to draw a horse like yours?" I nod, but I can't trust myself to speak because my throat's tight with emotion.

His father's eyes drop to my sketches once again and there's a long pause before he finally speaks. "Well, Toby clearly likes you, so how about I give you a two-week trial?"

I can't believe what I'm hearing. Relief, joy, gratitude - a mishmash of emotions - swirl inside me. I was convinced I wouldn't get the job, but now a huge smile bursts out of me.

"Thank you so much. I promise I won't let you down."

"I'll just need to take up a reference from your old job."

My smile instantly evaporates, and my cheeks burn with embarrassment at what I'm about to admit.

"I-I'm sorry there won't be a reference," my voice cracks because, however hard I try, I can't seem to catch a break.

"Why? What do you mean?" His eyes study me, taking in my flaming red cheeks and the fact I'm close to tears.

"I–I left my last job in a hurry. The lady I was looking after was lovely, but her husband–he–he wasn't a nice man." I finish feebly.

He frowns but seems to understand my inference. "Well, in that case, let's just see how we all get on over the next two weeks." His tone is matter-of-fact, and my body finally relaxes in relief.

"Toby, if you've finished, go up to your room and get ready for bed. You can choose a book to read, and I'll come up once I've cleared away."

"Thomas! Thomas! Thomas the Tank Engine!"

"Okay, but no more shouting." He grins, his face softening for the first time.

Toby scrambles down from the table and points at my sketches. "Can I keep these?" His eyes, the replica of his dad's, look at me shyly.

"Of course." I smile back, feeling ridiculously pleased.

As soon as Toby scampers out of the room, his father directs his gaze back at me. "Have you got anywhere to stay tonight?" I shake my head slowly. "Hmm, well, I guess you can move in now if you want. Take the weekend to settle in, and you can start properly on Monday morning. I'll show you to your room, and then I'll help you move your stuff in later."

The interview appears to be over, and we both stand up. Even though I'm sure it's wholly inappropriate for me to hug my new boss, I do it anyway.

"Thank you," I whisper into his hard chest before releasing him.

"By the way, you can call me Matt."

He gives me his first genuine smile since I arrived, and suddenly the dancing butterflies are back performing somersaults of joy, and I wonder if my luck has finally changed.

Chapter 2 – Matt

She certainly had balls…

I've just hired a nanny who has no experience and no reference. I must be losing it!

Rosie's clear blue eyes held mine head-on, as I'd glared down at her from the front door when she'd arrived. I'd towered over her small, slim frame but, despite giving her a scowl in welcome, she hadn't appeared intimidated at all by my obvious bad mood. Quite the opposite, in fact; she'd greeted me with a smile that lit up her open friendly face, and her eyes had danced with amusement.

I'd been beyond irritated by her lateness and instantly decided I'd no intention of giving her the job, so I'm not sure what made me change my mind. Maybe it was her quirky, funny sketches – she certainly had balls to draw a less than flattering caricature of me - or perhaps it was the immediate connection she and Toby seemed to share. It was a long time since I'd seen Toby so animated and enthusiastic and, while the nannies I'd previously employed had all been professional and kind, there was something different about Rosie that made me want to take a chance on employing her, despite her lack of qualifications or a reference.

From her C.V she's 26 years old, and she's had a series of temporary and dead-end jobs, mainly working in cafes, shops or cleaning. She's clearly a talented artist, and I wonder why she's only ever had short-term employment. Whatever the reason, Toby's enamoured with her and that's all that matters to me.

After Toby's bedtime and helping Rosie move her few possessions into her room, we make supper together. Rosie chats companionably, while I make a sauce for pasta, and then I open a bottle of wine that's been chilling in the fridge and hand her a glass. "Here's to your new job. I hope you'll enjoy looking after Toby and living here."

We clink glasses and Rosie smiles. "Thanks. I'm sure I'm going to love it here, and Toby's adorable. You must be so proud of him for coping with the loss of his mum." She stops abruptly, and her cheeks flood with colour. "I'm so sorry. I didn't mean to speak out of turn..." She trails off and bites down on her bottom lip, looking nervously at me.

"It's fine. Toby's been amazing, though she died when he was 2, so he doesn't have a strong memory of her."

"Does he ever talk about her?" she asks softly.

"Sometimes... I mean we don't '*not*' *t*alk about her. She'll always be his mum and part of us, but generally Toby's busy with all the things that 6-year-olds do, so it's not at the forefront of his mind, if you see what I mean." Rosie nods and I smile reassuringly at her, trying to ease the awkward moment.

"Do you mind me asking what happened? I mean, I quite understand if you'd rather not say."

"She died in a car accident," I tell her carefully, not offering any more details.

This is my sanitised version of events, which I use to make what happened palatable to people who are trying to be kind. The bare facts are that she died in a car accident and Toby was very young, but only a few trusted friends know the unadulterated truth. I've told Toby the barest details, which I've carefully censored because I'll always want him to think the best of his mum. Selfishly, I want him to think the best of me too, though I know I don't deserve it.

I'm relieved she now knows enough of what happened, so if Toby brings it up, she's prepared. My stomach tightens as the familiar sensations of regret and guilt well up inside me, and I decide I need something stronger than wine to dull my emotions. Turning away, I pour a Jameson whiskey, tasting the smooth, oaky flavour as it hits my throat.

Perhaps Rosie can tell that I don't want to talk about it anymore because she doesn't press me further but busies herself chopping ingredients for a salad. I watch her concentrating and feel the alcohol working, as my dark mood mellows. When the meal is ready, we sit at the kitchen table, and I explain my and Toby's work and school routine.

"I just need you to be here when I can't be. School drop-off and pickups, of course, and organising Toby's school uniform and after-school activities, and anything else he needs. I usually have breakfast with him, but I can't always be back in time in the evening if there's a problem at the centre. Mrs B comes in twice a week to clean, but I'll need you to be flexible, so the house runs smoothly." I finish and look at Rosie, who's nodding.

"Of course."

"I'm sure we can fit in with each other. I'll show you around the Equestrian Centre tomorrow and also where Toby's primary school is, so you can get your bearings."

After dinner, I make us both mugs of coffee. It's a warm evening, and Rosie takes hers and wanders through the open glass doors onto the patio and sits on one of the wooden chairs. The brightness from the kitchen is enough, but I light one of the terracotta candles on the patio table anyway, and we sit companionably drinking our coffee and gazing out into the garden. The moonlight casts soft, silvery shadows across the lawn and, from the fields beyond, intermittent nocturnal sounds punctuate the peacefulness.

"I love this time of the day," she murmurs softly.

Her eyes capture mine and her face lights up with happiness. She looks beautiful, and I feel myself spontaneously smiling back. A surprising furl of peace unwraps itself inside me, and I tentatively test out the unfamiliar sensation. It feels wrong. Emotions I always keep carefully guarded and under control suddenly threaten to spill out of me, and I swallow them down hard, my chest tightening with the effort of trying to dispel them.

"You should go to your room and get settled in." My voice sounds brusquer than I intend and, after she leaves, I rebuke myself for my surliness. After all, she was only trying to be friendly.

Chapter 3 – Rosie

I've literally got stupid horse envy!

Matt was good company over dinner, with no sign of his sour mood from when I'd first arrived. As he owns a riding centre, I'd assumed horses would be the main topic of conversation; not ideal, as I know nothing about them. Perhaps Matt realised because instead we talked about Toby; his daily routine and his likes and dislikes. Diplomatically, he also stayed off the awkward topic of my last job and, after my gruelling day travelling, I was grateful for that.

There was one awkward moment when I tactlessly brought up Matt's late wife, and instantly a shadow of pain creased his face. Even though four years have passed, I know more than most that grief isn't time-limited, and I berate myself for being insensitive. He clearly loved his wife very much, and the agony of losing her and the grief he now bears breaks my heart. I feel awful for Toby too; to lose his mum at such a tender, age is cruel beyond words, and I make a promise to myself that I'll do whatever I can to make him happy in my role as his new nanny.

After saying goodnight to Matt, I sleep like a proverbial log; heavy and dreamless, waking to the incessant sound of my alarm clock. Sunlight streams in from my open bedroom window, and I stretch out lazily beneath my soft white duvet, listening to the whinnying sound of horses in the fields outside.

My room is simply furnished, but it's comfortable. Besides the double bed, there's a small bedside table, a matching chest of drawers, and a wardrobe. The walls are painted plain white, and there are a couple of soft rugs on the oak wood flooring. A comfy armchair and television mounted on the wall completes the room. I also have my own ensuite bathroom. After my inauspicious start with Matt, I'm so grateful to be here, enveloped in warmth and happiness and, not only that, I feel safe.

My mind drifts back over the last few years and the sorrow I'd felt for so much of it. I'd hoped the job in Cornwall would be the fresh start I badly needed, but that hadn't worked out, and I shudder as I recall Jackson's unwanted advances. Yet, walking into the kitchen yesterday, something had resonated deep within me. It was as if I'd finally come home. I almost laugh out loud. This is a job, pure and simple, and I need to make sure I don't screw it up.

After breakfast, including the disgustingly strong coffee that Matt thinks I like, the day passes in a blur of sights, people and information, as he and Toby take me on a tour of the Equestrian Centre. Matt explains the centre provides riding lessons for all abilities, with a range of qualifications, and the opportunity to train for show jumping competitions and cross-country events. As well as a riding school and an all-weather training arena, there are livery facilities, all surrounded by 60 acres of land.

As we enter one of the stable blocks, Matt takes a carrot from his pocket and offers it to a sleek black stallion looking at us inquisitively over the gate.

"This is Thunder. He's been with me for 5 years now."

I watch in fascination as Matt talks softly to Thunder, and the horse nuzzles the top of his chest in response. There seems to be a natural bond between them, as he continues to engage gently with the stallion. He's more relaxed than I've ever seen him, his face stress-free and happy, in stark contrast to the tension and seriousness I've witnessed until now. It's obvious how important horses are to his well-being. My heart does a little belly flop, as I observe this complex man come alive in the environment he loves best.

Matt's biceps stretch the cotton material of his black T-shirt, as he burrows his fingers into Thunder's mane. *What wouldn't I give to be Thunder!* I shake my head at how ridiculous I'm being. *I've literally got stupid horse envy!* Hastily, I tear my eyes away, trying to pull myself together, and notice Toby staring up in awe at his dad.

"I think you've got another budding rider in the family." I grin at Toby.

Matt looks down at his son and laughs. "You want to pat Thunder, buddy?"

Toby nods shyly, and Matt gently lifts his young son in his strong, muscular arms. Toby keeps one arm firmly around Matt's neck and leans forward with his other hand to lightly touch Thunder's forelock. All the time, Matt talks quietly and encouragingly, and Toby slowly loosens his vice-like grip on Matt's neck, as he becomes more confident being near the large animal. Thunder stands steadily, every so often slowly swishing his head, as Toby tentatively strokes him.

My breath catches in my throat as I absorb this beautifully tender father and son moment, and I take a snapshot in my mind so I can capture it in a sketch when we get home.

Chapter 4 – Matt

What did the horse say...?

It's interesting to see the centre through Rosie's eyes, especially as she tells me she's never ridden a horse before. I introduce her to some of the stable grooms and then to my secretary, Hannah, who runs the office. Finally, she meets Harry, my stable manager and best friend. She watches us in amusement as Harry and I banter with each other, and I notice him eyeing up Rosie in her tight jeans and tee. He obviously likes what he sees. Harry was always a player and a flirt, and I'd be worried if I didn't know how happy he is with his girlfriend, Caz. All the same, I glare pointedly, making it clear to him that Rosie's out of bounds.

Harry brushes off my scowl and bends down to pull Toby up onto his broad shoulders. Toby loves Harry and giggles excitedly, breaking any awkwardness.

"Harry's an Aussie," I tell Rosie. "We met when I was travelling around Queensland, and we were both working on a cattle station. It wasn't glamorous — mostly mucking out and feeding — but sometimes we got to ride young and inexperienced horses, which are called 'green' horses over there. Then Harry turned up here one day needing a job, and I felt sorry for him."

Harry raises his eyebrows at me and laughs. "More like I took pity on you."

It's true. Harry's equine skill and experience have been indispensable to the success of the centre, and I know I couldn't have achieved as much without him. He's been my stalwart friend for 10 years and his unfailing support, especially when I'd been at my lowest, means I'd do anything for this burly giant of a man.

We stroll over to the paddock and watch several horses being put through their paces by the stable lads. Toby's still sitting on Harry's strong shoulders and Rosie gives him her undivided attention as he fires out a stream of questions at her. Not once does she show any impatience or frustration at Toby's incessant chit-chat. Quite the opposite; she's patient and kind, engaging with him fully and returning her own questions so that his adoring eyes remain transfixed on her, as if she's his very own superhero. He's clearly got a little crush on her but then there's something about Rosie – the way she smiles, the way she tilts her head when she's thinking, the soft lilt of her voice – there's natural warmth and lightness about her and it's obvious that Harry's just as captivated as Toby.

Rosie comes to stand next to me, her bare brown arms resting against the fence. I'm half-listening to the conversation, but then her soft, musical laughter pulls me back into her bright orbit. She's reacting to something Harry's just said and the sound's infectious and full of goodness, just like her. It's also oddly overwhelming and I take a deep, steadying breath before moving a step away to put some distance between us.

Rosie suddenly looks over at me and grins. "What did the horse say when it fell?" I raise an eyebrow at her. "I've fallen and I can't giddyup!" She falls about laughing.

I exaggerate a loud groan but can't help laughing back.

"I have another one." She smirks. "What happened to the man who owned a riding school?" She looks straight at me, her blue eyes dancing with amusement. "Business kept falling off!"

Harry and Toby giggle as I pretend to grimace.

"Rosie, these jokes are awful." Harry guffaws loudly.

"One more." She sniggers. "Where do horses go when they're sick?" She pauses for dramatic effect. "The horsepital!"

"NO MORE!" We all chorus in unison and Rosie makes a deep theatrical bow as if she's just finished performing at a smash-hit comedy gig.

"We should go before Rosie cracks any more cheesy jokes." I tease.

Rosie's eyes meet mine; her cheeks are flushed pink, and the sun captures the golden highlights in her hair. She looks beautiful and a dull ache of longing settles in my chest, taking me by surprise. I clamp down hard on my jaw, trying to switch off whatever this unsettling feeling is. I'm always in control and yet, at this precise moment, I'm anything but. A strand of hair has fallen over her face and it takes everything I've got not to reposition it back behind her ear. I clench my palms into tight fists and force my eyes away before walking purposefully back towards the house.

Chapter 5 – Rosie

Oh no, not more coffee…

Matt's pride in his riding centre is clear to see. There was a friendly and efficient working atmosphere, and the stable lads seemed to admire and respect both Matt and Harry. They're obviously best friends, and I'm intrigued to know more about how they met in Australia and how Harry came to be working for Matt. However, I don't want to come across as being nosy, so I decide to save my questions for another time.

After our tour of the centre, we drive to the nearby pretty yellow-stone Cotswold village, where Toby's primary school is, so I can see where I do the school drop offs and pickups. We park and have a leisurely stroll around the village green and every so often someone will come up to Matt to pass the time of day; he seems popular and well liked. There's a thatched roofed pub, post office/general store and several gift shops, but we head towards a small café which has an enclosed garden with outside seating and tables under brightly coloured parasols.

Matt orders our food and we sit outside in the warm spring sunshine, chatting easily as we eat lunch. Pale pink cherry blossom carpets the grass from where it's fallen from an overladen tree and a surge of happiness bubbles up inside me as I take a sneaky sideways peek at Matt through my sunglasses. His long legs are stretched out in front of him as he lounges back in his chair, while answering what seems like Toby's one hundredth 'why' question today. Matt must see me looking at him because he suddenly sits up and winks.

"Toby, how about an ice-cream?"

"Yeeeees!" Toby exclaims excitedly.

Matt grins wickedly at me and I cotton on immediately that it's the perfect way to distract Toby from his endless stream of questions – at least for a few minutes.

They both disappear inside to buy ice-cream for Toby and more coffees for us, and I sigh inwardly at the thought of the strong unpleasant drink I'm going to have to swallow. I really should tell Matt that I don't like coffee, but now it feels awkward admitting it. He loves the stuff and assumes I do too, but the only way it's palatable is if I put tons of sugar in it and then it tastes syrupy and not so bitter.

Just as we're leaving, I notice a woman waving enthusiastically at us from across the road. We walk over and she hugs Matt and Toby affectionately. She's probably in her late 60's with a face that looks used to laughing and warm, twinkling eyes that instantly make me like her.

"This is Mrs B." Matt introduces us both, smiling. "She looks after us; we couldn't do without her."

"Aww, don't be silly." Mrs B gives Matt a wide smile and reaches out to clasp my hand. "I'm so pleased to meet you, Rosie. I clean at the house on Mondays and Fridays, so we're bound to see each other. Maybe we can have a coffee together next time I'm there and get to know each other."

I nod, smiling back. "I'd love that." *Oh no, not more coffee, I grimace inside.*

Chapter 6 – Rosie

That's not in my job description.

Toby looks so sweet in his smart green school uniform and it's adorable to see him run enthusiastically into the playground to greet his friends. I linger for a moment or two at the school gate watching him playing before making my way back to my car through the throng of mainly mums who are chatting together in small groups.

I stop off on the way home to do a big supermarket shop at the out-of-town store and when I get home, Mrs B's sitting at the kitchen table drinking coffee.

"Rosie, how lovely to see you again," she gets up and embraces me in a big hug.

"You too," I reply, switching on the kettle to make myself a mug of tea.

We chat amiably while I unpack the food shopping and then Mrs B goes back to whatever she'd been doing, while I go up to Toby's room to change his bed and tidy his room.

The time passes quickly and soon Mrs B breaks for lunch and I join her for a sandwich.

She's a smiley, friendly woman who clearly adores Matt and Toby, and the conversation between us flows easily. She explains she's lived in the village all her life and is married to Mr B, who's retired, and who sometimes helps Matt with maintenance jobs in the yard if needed. The 'B' is obviously a shortened version of their surname, and I wonder if it's been like that for so long now that no one either knows or cares what the original surname is.

"I've got so many entertaining stories about Toby." Mrs B breaks into my thoughts, and I focus back on what she's saying. "He must have been about 3 years old, and he was enjoying helping me with some housework, as little ones like to do. Except, his version of helping was to 'tidy up' his dad's things. I felt bad about that because, after Toby fell asleep, it took Matt all evening to find his wallet and keys."

"Poor Matt, I can imagine him turning the house upside down and all his frustration." I chuckle.

"Then another time, Matt left his laptop open and somehow Toby accidentally deleted a very important spreadsheet. I mean, it was an accident, but Matt was a little tetchy over that."

"Oh no. Still, it wasn't wise to leave it open with a toddler around," I commiserate.

"No, well, he learnt his lesson the hard way. Oh, I've just remembered another one. One day, Toby was eating a banana in the kitchen and his dad came in and asked if he was enjoying it. Toby replied in a perfectly deadpan voice, 'It's too small. I want a big banana, like yours.' Well, at that point, we both knew Toby wasn't talking about bananas!"

I burst out laughing and store that little nugget away to tease Matt about. Maybe it's too soon though, and I need to get to know him better.

Mrs B regards me thoughtfully. "If you ever need me to have Toby for an hour or two in the day, don't hesitate to ask. I could have him to stay overnight too, if Matt's got an event he wants to take you to."

I sit up in surprise, not because it isn't kind of Mrs B to offer, but because she's talking as if Matt and I are a couple, and I'm not simply the nanny. It would be part of my job to look after Toby if Matt wanted to go out one evening, but I thank her all the same and then idly daydream about what sort of date Matt might take me on, but then I come to my senses. Even if Matt wasn't still mourning his late wife, he wouldn't be interested in me.

***

I'm back at the school gate mid-afternoon to collect Toby from school, and on a whim, I decide we'll go to the nearby play park, so he can run off some steam.

I make myself comfortable on the park bench which is dedicated to 'Joan and Alan who loved to spend time here' and watch as Toby tries out first the small slide and then the swings. The equipment looks well-maintained and safe, but I don't take my eyes off him in case he needs me.

I'm just thinking of heading home when a young woman walks over and sits down next to me. Her appearance is striking; almost jet-black hair streaked with purple, thick kohl eyeliner, a boho-chic style dress and white Doc Martin boots.

"Hi, are you Toby's new nanny?" She smiles uncertainly at me, and when I nod, she extends her hand. "I thought you might be. I'm Caz, Harry's girlfriend from the stables."

"It's great to meet you." I return her smile and notice she's around my age.

"I was hoping to bump into you. How are you getting on?" Her smoky eyes are welcoming and immediately put me at ease.

"Fine, though it's only my first official day, really. I'm on a two-week trial, so fingers crossed it'll go okay."

"I'm sure it will. Matt's great when you get to know him, and Toby's just gorgeous."

"Yes, Toby's lovely. Umm... how long have you known Matt?"

"Oh, let's see... when I started going out with Harry, so nearly 2 years. Matt and Harry are best friends, so they hang out a lot together. Look, I have to scoot now, but if you're around tomorrow morning after school drop-off, we could have a coffee, and I'll fill you in on all the gossip." Caz winks at me.

"I'd love that."

Caz waves goodbye to Toby, and after she leaves, I sit a while longer contemplating our brief conversation. I'm touched that she came over to introduce herself and maybe tomorrow she'll tell me more about Matt's friendship with Harry. And since I don't know anyone else in the village, it would be great if we could become friends.

***

The next morning when I drop Toby off, Caz is waiting for me at the school gate, and she introduces me to one of the mums she knows.

"This is Janine. Her son, Olly, and Toby are in the same class," she explains. "Janine and I got to know each other because we moved into the village at a similar time. It's a friendly little community, and everyone looks out for each other."

Janine gazes at me shyly. "Hi, pleased to meet you."

She looks a little younger than me, and I have the impression that Caz has taken her under her wing. "Toby's been talking a lot about Olly." I smile, trying to break the ice. "He says Olly's his 'bestest' friend in the entire world."

"Ha, yes, Olly loves Toby too... umm, maybe Toby would like to come for a playdate after school tomorrow? Olly's been on about having him around for ages... I could give them tea."

"That's a great idea. I'm sure he'd love that."

We exchange contact details and the time I should collect Toby. A little frisson of happiness buzzes through me, as I think about Toby's reaction when I tell him he's got a playdate with his best friend.

***

After leaving Janine, Caz and I make our way over to the same café Matt took me to a couple of days earlier. It's another warm day, and we sit outside enjoying the spring sunshine. Thankfully, I can drink my favourite builder's tea today, and we order freshly baked scones to go with our drinks.

"This is the life." Caz stretches out in her seat and sighs.

"I know it's great. Do you have the day off today?"

"I work for myself, so my hours are pretty flexible. I've got my own jewellery-making business, and I'm a singer/songwriter. If you want a singer for a birthday party or wedding, I'm your girl."

"Gosh, you sound busy."

"Well, the singing isn't regular. I'd like to do more but…" She shrugs. "The jewellery business is doing ok, though. I sell through the gift shop in the village, so have a browse next time you're in."

"I will - thanks. So, how did you meet Harry?"

"At the pub." She laughs. "I'd just moved into my flat in the village, and Harry offered to come over and put up some shelves. Classic chat up line, huh! Anyway, we've been together ever since, and I moved in with him about a year ago." Her face clouds over. "I'm just scared he'll decide to go back to Oz one day."

"Do you think he will?"

"I really don't know. We don't talk about it much, but he has parents there, so… "

I take a sip of my tea and decide to change the subject.

"Tell me about Matt? I know his wife died in a car accident, but that's about it."

"Yeah, Harry had only come here for the summer but, when the accident happened, he took over the day-to-day running of the centre so that Matt could concentrate on Toby. I think Harry pretty much got Matt through it all. Then Matt offered Harry a full-time manager's job at the centre and so he stayed on.

"It's so sad," I say quietly.

Caz looks at me carefully. "Have you met Belle yet?"

"Toby mentioned someone called Belle, but no, I haven't."

"I'm sure you will soon. She's Matt's girlfriend."

I feel my cheeks colour as I'm caught off-guard. I hadn't once considered that Matt might have a girlfriend. "Oh, okay. Are they serious?"

"Belle certainly has ambitions to become the next Mrs O'Connell for sure, though Harry thinks Matt's not interested in being in a serious relationship again. Anyway, Belle's the least maternal person I've ever met. She'd probably send Toby off to boarding school the first opportunity she got."

"You're kidding?" I ask incredulously.

"You'll see for yourself soon enough." She laughs hollowly. "Belle's very career focused. She runs her own swanky interior design company in London, but she comes up for the weekend now and again to see Matt."

It's ridiculous that my stomach sinks at the thought of Matt being in a relationship. His wife died 4 years ago, so it's perfectly reasonable that he would be involved with someone by now; he's an attractive man in his 30's after all. Even so, I can't believe he'd want to be with someone who'd consider sending his son away to boarding school.

A snapshot pops into my head of Matt reading a bedtime story to Toby last night. I'd been en route to my room but stood transfixed in the open doorway, as I'd listened to him acting out the voices of the Thomas the Tank Engine characters. Toby was completely entranced as his father brought the story to life. Matt's a wonderful father, and he and Toby are so close it would be awful if that changed because of his relationship with Belle.

Then again, Matt has suffered the unimaginable pain of losing his young wife. He deserves a girlfriend who makes him happy, and I should be pleased for him.

"All I care about is Toby's well-being." I lie, *because, as much as I don't want to admit it, I'm starting to care about Matt's well-being too, and that's not in my job description.*

Chapter 7 – Rosie

Make sure she's not an axe murderer…

I'd meant to tell Matt about Toby's playdate last night, but it slipped my mind. Then I was going to tell him at breakfast, but he was on an early shift at the stables and wasn't back by the time we left for school. I'm sure it doesn't matter. The main thing is that Toby's excited about seeing Olly after school, and he'll be eager to tell his dad all about it when he gets back this evening.

After dropping off Toby at school, I wander into the village to find the gift shop where Caz sells her handmade jewellery. The shop is jam-packed with the usual trinkets and knick-knacks aimed at tourists. But there are also handcrafted cards and pottery by local artists and locally made chutney, jams and biscuits. I spend a while happily browsing before choosing a pair of simple rose-gold hoop earrings from Caz's range of jewellery.

She's so talented, and I make a mental note to tell her how exquisite and original her designs are. That happens sooner than I expect because, as I'm leaving the shop, I see her walking along the high street, and I hurry over the road to greet her.

"Look what I've just bought." I take out the small gift bag and show her the delicate earrings in the box. "I love them."

"Ah, I'm so glad. But next time tell me what you want, and I'll make a bespoke piece for you and, even better, I'll give you a friend's discount." Caz grins at me.

We chat for a while longer but we've both got errands to run so, after a few minutes, we say our goodbyes and reluctantly head in opposite directions. No café break for us this morning. Still, I decide, I really like Caz. She's friendly and easy to talk to, and she makes beautiful jewellery.

***

By school pickup time, I'm curled up on one of the wingback chairs, savouring the peacefulness and quiet of the kitchen without Toby in it. The afternoon sun streams through the open glass patio doors, bathing me in gentle comforting warmth, while I sketch a simple pencil drawing of Matt and Toby. After tea last night, they'd watched a funny cartoon, giggling together at some silly joke, and then just before bedtime, Matt had listened to Toby reading from his school book. Whatever they do together, it's obvious they adore one another, and I want to capture their special connection in my sketch.

Matt's face is in profile; his eyes focused on Toby as he reads. I've subtly shaded Toby's delicate features as he glances up to meet his father's eyes and there's a pure, unguarded moment of love between them. There's something else too; a strong, unbreakable bond through their shared grief, perhaps? I'm pleased with my sketch and, as I concentrate, a swathe of contentment relaxes me because I love it here. Then Matt strolls in.

He scans the kitchen, which I have to say looks unusually tidy because Toby's not here. After a moment, he looks over at me and I quickly close my pad, so he won't see my sketch.

"Where's Toby?" His eyes look at me questioningly.

"He's on a playdate." I smile back reassuringly.

Matt's face clouds over; his features tensing. He walks towards me, eating up the space between us in three strides and I'm suddenly in the shadow of his tall frame as it towers over me. I take a nervous swallow, feeling at a disadvantage as I'm still sitting, and look up into his eyes as they scrutinise me.

"What the hell's a playdate?"

"You know, playing after school and having tea."

"Playing with whom?" he snaps out the words.

"He's with Olly, his friend from school." I tense as Matt's eyes continue to drill into mine.

"So, he's with some random person I've never met."

"He's with Olly and Janine, his mum," I say evenly. "She offered to host a playdate and I'm collecting him in half an hour."

"Jesus, Rosie, how well do you know this woman?"

"Caz introduced us. She's a mum from school, and Toby and Olly are best friends. I haven't done a police check, if that's what you mean."

"I can't believe you didn't ask me. How the hell do we know he's safe?" Matt glares at me angrily, a muscle pulsating in his cheek.

"I..." I begin, but he cuts me off and abruptly walks out of the kitchen, slamming the door to his office as he goes inside.

I stare after him, my heart pumping furiously against my rib cage. What on earth was that about? Yes, I should have checked with him first but, even so, his reaction was totally over the top - wasn't it? Doubt settles uneasily in my stomach as I brood over Matt's behaviour.

***

After a minute, I tentatively knock on Matt's office door and go in. Matt's standing looking out of the window, his back muscles rigid and tense.

"I'm sorry," I say quietly. "I should have run it by you."

He turns to face me, his eyes dark and shadowed and his expression showing none of the friendliness from the last few days, "Yes, you should."

"Look, why don't you come with me to pick Toby up and you can check out Olly's mum and make sure she's not an axe murderer?" I say flippantly, hoping to lighten his mood.

"Are you trying to be funny?" But his face relaxes slightly.

On the journey over, Matt's eyes focus on the road as he manoeuvres his 4x4 skilfully down the narrow country lanes leading to the village. He's a capable driver, and my eyes automatically drift over to his rolled-up shirt sleeves which show off his strong tanned forearms and then down to his muscular thighs wrapped in dark denim. Though he's no longer angry, there's still tension in his eyes, and I want more than anything to reach out to him. He's just trying to be a good father and maybe he's a little over-protective, but that's only because Toby's lost his mum. I heave out a sigh and drag my eyes back up. Matt's intent on ignoring me and so I stare out of the window for the rest of the drive, ignoring him too.

As we get out of the car, children's excited laughter floats over from Janine's back-garden. She must have seen us arrive, because she greets us from the garden gate and ushers us in.

"This is Matt, Toby's dad," I say, introducing them, and I'm relieved when Matt walks over to Janine, his face smiling and friendly, to shake her hand.

She greets us both and leads us into the small, enclosed back-garden which is mainly grassed with neatly planted borders around the edges. We all watch as Toby and Olly gallop around, snorting and neighing, pretending to be horses. It's obvious they're having fun, both of them laughing hysterically at each other.

"They've had a picnic and ice cream – not very healthy, I'm afraid." Janine looks up at Matt shyly and he grins back.

"That's very kind of you. Thanks for having Toby for a playdate…umm…would Olly like to come over next week to play?"

Janine nods happily and I let out a shaky breath; one that I seem to have held in since we arrived. I have a sudden urge to poke Matt in the chest at his ridiculous behaviour earlier, but then, to add insult to injury, he says, "I think regular playdates with Olly are a great idea."

Toby spends the drive home chatting non-stop about his playdate. He's buzzing with excitement, and I can't help feeling a little bit smug about that. But after he's in bed, I head to my room for the rest of the evening. I've had enough of Mr Moody for one day.

***

There's a gentle knock on my bedroom door and I sigh huffily, putting down my unfinished sketch. I really hope Matt's not here to lecture me again about Toby's playdate.

"Hi, I came to apologise for how I behaved earlier. I'm probably a little overprotective of Toby, but I know I overreacted." He grins at me sheepishly, and I notice he's got a full-on 5-o'clock shadow, which is actually a sexy 9-o'clock one, as he scrapes his hand through his thick brown hair, looking embarrassed.

"It's my fault. I should have asked you first… but he needs to play with friends his own age," I say quickly, before I lose my courage.

"Yes, I know. I just need to get used to the idea, I suppose. Anyway, I'm very sorry about earlier."

There's strain on his face and a fragility about him that makes me want to reach out and hug him. Instead, I bite down on my bottom lip, trying to think of something to say to ease the awkwardness between us.

"Look, I promise I'll run it by you next time…umm…why don't we have a glass of wine to celebrate Toby's first proper playdate?"

Trying to diffuse the tension, I give him a hesitant smile, but when he doesn't reply, I slip past him and downstairs to the kitchen. I'm pouring wine into my glass when Matt puts his hand over the top of his.

"Thanks, but I think I need something stronger." His eyes catch mine for a moment and his face relaxes a little as he pours whiskey for himself. "I should have trusted you," he murmurs so quietly I wonder if he's talking to himself.

The oaky aroma from the whiskey and Matt's lemony aftershave lingers in the air between us and my eyelids flutter close as I breathe in the smell. It embodies everything about him; it's strong and masculine and gorgeous... a lethal combination. We're so close; almost touching, and my eyes drift slowly from his face to his broad shoulders and then down to his chest beneath his shirt. As he lifts his glass to mine, our fingers briefly brush together and a powerful tsunami of desire, like an electric current, sparks around my body. It's so intense, I'm certain Matt must feel it too, and I take a step back to create some space between us.

"Here's to trust," I say quickly, not daring to meet his eyes in case he can read what I'm thinking, as we clink glasses together.

Chapter 8 – Rosie

Daddy says mummy loves them…

There's something compelling about Matt. Certainly, he's attractive, his dark looks making him easy on the eye, but it's much more than that.

Maybe it's his passion and energy for the riding centre and the horses in his care, or the way his enthusiasm rubs off on Toby. It's even beginning to rub off on me a little too, though I'm not prepared to test his notion that I'd enjoy riding.

Perhaps it's because he spends as much time with Toby as he can, both of them often lying stretched out on Toby's bedroom floor, building Lego or playing with 'Thomas' trains, or simply chatting about Toby's day. His love for his young son shines through in everything they do together.

Then there's Matt's fierce protectiveness of Toby, like yesterday when he'd struggled to hold his emotions in when I'd arranged a playdate with someone he didn't know. Imagine having someone care so much about your well-being; to always have your back. It would be incredible to be loved like that.

I stare despondently at the mirror in my ensuite and frown, my sleepless night showing in the dark shadows under my eyes. I can't deny my burgeoning feelings for Matt. But, in the wise morning light, I resolve to ignore them, because he's not only my boss, he's also involved with someone else. She must be special... she's lucky, too.

I'm the unlucky one.

I allow myself one last moment of quiet reflection. Then I reluctantly dismiss Matt from my thoughts and walk purposefully along to Toby's room to wake him.

***

Toby and Olly come running out of school at pickup time, while I stand chatting to Janine, and I suggest that we all go to the park for a while so the boys can play. Janine seems grateful for the suggestion, and we sit together on a bench, ('in memory of Jack Goodman, a dear friend') watching the boys laughing and racing around with each other.

We chat idly for a few minutes, and I find out that Janine is 22 years old and a single mum.

"It's so lovely that Olly has someone to play with," she says quietly.

"Same for Toby... they're having lots of fun together." I laugh as I watch the boys careering down the play slide and then immediately climb back up again.

Janine looks at me shyly and I can see some hesitation in her eyes before she says, "I wonder if you'd mind reading something for me. I'm not very good at reading and I've had a letter from my landlord. I'm scared he's giving me notice or something." Janine's cheeks flush pink, and I rush to reassure her.

"Of course, no problem… let's see what the letter says." She takes out an envelope from her bag and hands it to me. "It's just asking you when it would be convenient for him to come round to paint your kitchen. He says he can come next Friday or the following Wednesday, if it suits you better."

"Oh, thank you so much. I've been so worried about what the letter says."

"There's a phone number you can ring and tell him which day you would like."

"I'll ring him when we get home. Thanks," she says again.

"It must be difficult for you if you find reading hard," I say carefully.

"I just never got the hang of it when I was at school, and now I'm struggling to help Olly when he brings books home to read from his teacher."

"I'd be happy to help you if you'd like?" I offer, hoping she won't be offended.

"Would you really?"

"Yes, of course. My brother struggled a bit with reading and writing at school, and then he was diagnosed with dyslexia. He sometimes got his letters mixed up, and I used to help him."

Janine's eyes have welled up and are threatening to spill over with tears. I reach out for her hand and squeeze it, wanting to comfort her. "Maybe we can read one of Olly's books together. I'm sure it won't be long before you feel a bit more confident."

I'm pleased Janine has confided in me, and we arrange a time when we can meet up the following week for our first reading session together. I also decide to look at local adult literacy classes, though Janine might need some convincing on that idea.

***

After we leave the park and say goodbye to Janine and Olly, Toby pulls on my hand. "What's up, Toby?" I ask.

"Can we go to see mummy in the churchyard, please?"

"Yes, of course, sweetheart. You'll have to show me where she is, though."

Toby and I stroll towards the beautiful old church which is set above a slight incline at the end of the village. We walk through the black iron gate and up a sweeping tarmac drive which is lined with needle-sharp conifers, before reaching the neatly kept graveyard. Toby turns off the main driveway onto a narrow gravel path that leads to the Garden of Remembrance and, to the left, some newer gravestones.

"This is mummy." Toby points to the grave and then kneels on the grass and traces the outline of the words on the gravestone with his finger.

Sara Elizabeth O'Connell (née Bailey)
Dearly loved daughter, wife and mother
5.8.1988 – 7.9.2019
'Fly Free'

Underneath the inscription, there's a simple drawing of some sunflowers and a butterfly which are all set into the shiny black granite. "I drew those," Toby announces proudly. "Daddy says mummy loves them."

I can't help the tears pooling in my eyes at the unfairness of Toby losing his mum at such a young age. I gulp down hard and force a smile. "They're beautiful, sweetie. I'm sure your mummy really loves them."

We sit for a while enjoying the peacefulness of the churchyard, a loudly chirping robin, the only sound interrupting the quietness. The late afternoon sun is warm and comforting against my skin and my mind drifts to something my mum used to say: 'Loved ones are near when robins appear'. Many people take comfort in believing that a robin is a sign that a loved one is visiting them, and I wonder if Sara's keeping a watchful eye on her young son because, as far-fetched as it sounds, I know I have my own guardian angel in heaven looking after me.

Toby crouches by his mum's stone and I sit on a nearby bench ('in memory of Annie Cooper, a friend to all') while I listen as he tells his mum about all the important things he's been doing lately like stroking Thunder at the stables and playing with his best friend, Olly. It's a beautiful, tender moment as I watch a little boy simply chatting to his mum. He was just 2 years old when she died, yet I can see there's a touching connection between them and that surely must be because of Matt's influence and selfless love for his son.

How different Toby's life would be if his mum had lived. He'll never know her loving touch whenever he wakes at night from a bad dream or grazes his knee. She'll never be at his school concert or his wedding. My heart breaks for all that he's lost. As for Matt, he wears his grief like an iron mask bolted to his face, his pain impenetrable. Sadly, I know that Matt's loss is immeasurable, as is my own.

Chapter 9 – Matt

You'll have to find a gentle old granny horse…

I'm an expert at keeping my feelings bolted down, except where Toby's concerned. Yesterday I'd panicked at the thought that he was with someone I didn't know. It wasn't until I saw him playing happily in Janine's garden with his friend Olly that my heart settled into its regular beat in my chest, and I realised how unreasonably I'd behaved. After Toby had gone to bed, I'd apologised to Rosie for my overreaction and, being the kind natured girl that she is, we'd ended the night back to being friends again. Rosie makes my boy happy, and I can't lose her because of my stupid trust issues. Sometimes I overhear her and Toby laughing or singing together, and I know how lucky we are to have her here, making life so much better than it was before.

I plan on asking Rosie to go riding with me today because it seems absurd that she lives next to my Equestrian Centre and yet she's never even been on a horse. My whole life revolves around horses, and I want her to have a better insight into what Harry and I do. However, when I broach the subject at breakfast, she's less than enthusiastic.

"Honestly, Rosie, it'll be fun." I try to sound encouraging.

"Really, I'm not sure it will." She doesn't make any effort to hide her obvious reluctance.

"Look, we'll just have a short ride out and if you really hate it, I promise I won't make you do it again."

"Okay, but you'll have to find a gentle old granny horse for me."

Her eyes land on mine and I can't help smirking. "I don't have any old granny horses, but I'll find a placid one for you. Come up to the stables when you get back from dropping Toby off at school and we'll go out then."

***

"This is Daisy. She's a 4-year-old mare, and she's very good-natured and used to the mounting block." I pat Daisy on her forelock and smile encouraging at Rosie.

"I'll make sure the reins are secure - right, so step onto the mounting block like this, and rest your hand here. Your other hand should be on the other side of the saddle. Try to even your weight over the centre of the horse... left foot in the strap – knees facing forward. Balance over the horse and swing your leg over the saddle. Then just sit until you have your balance."

To be on the safe side, I've got Liam, one of the stable grooms, on the other side of the mare to help just in case Rosie somehow takes a flying leap and falls off. I'm impressed though, because she sets her mouth in a determined line of concentration and mounts effortlessly.

"Well done, that's brilliant."

She still looks nervous, but after a few more minutes of further instruction, I feel confident enough to lead her into the training field. We practise several more mounts and dismounts without the block and also how to use the reins correctly.

"How about we ride up towards that copse of trees and back?" I point to a sloping incline in the distance.

Rosie nods and I mount my horse and lead us off slowly, making sure I keep a careful watch on her. While she's a little less tense than earlier, she's completely focused on riding, so I decide not to distract her by talking.

It doesn't take us long to reach the small area of trees at the highest point of my land, and I quickly dismount and assist Rosie to do the same. We leave the horses grazing and walk the short distance to the brow of the hill so we can sit and admire the view; a patchwork of green and brown palette fields and what appear like tiny scale-model Cotswold villages in the distance.

"Is the view worth it?" I look at her, trying to gauge her reaction to the ride.

"Oh yes, definitely." Rosie smiles, her face relaxing for the first time since we set off.

"I was worried you'd hate it." I grin.

"Well, I wasn't keen on the idea, but now I'm glad I've done it." There's pride in her voice and, for some reason, I feel ridiculously pleased, though why it matters to me, I don't know.

It's another beautiful day and we lapse into an easy silence, the late morning sunshine warming us as we continue to stare out at the sweeping landscape.

"Toby took me to see his mum in the churchyard yesterday. I hope you don't mind?" Her eyes look questioningly at me as she nervously bites down on her bottom lip.

"No, of course not - he likes to go sometimes. Did he show you the sunflowers and butterfly he drew?"

Rosie nods, smiling. "It was lovely. He told her all the things he'd been doing." She hesitates. "I can't imagine how awful it must have been when she died."

I want to close the conversation down, but for some reason, I don't. I continue staring at the view, even though I feel Rosie's eyes on me. "Everyone always assumes we were happy." My voice sounds hoarse, and my next words escape my lips without me even realising. "Sara was leaving me and Toby."

I wonder if I've made her feel uncomfortable, and I wait for some placatory expression of sympathy, but instead she asks, "How did you meet Sara?"

I clench my jaw and swallow down hard. "We met at university. She was a year older than me, but she stayed on to do her Masters, while I finished my degree."

I trail off for a moment, because my throat is thick with emotion. "She was a real party girl, always popular and fun to be with. We just clicked. Then when we'd both finished university, we went travelling for a few months... India, Vietnam and we ended up in Australia. Sara hated it - the food, the heat, the travelling – and she was homesick. So, when we got to Australia, she flew back home, but I stayed on, and that's when I met Harry."

I never talk about Sara, yet now I can't stop the words tumbling out of me.

"I thought we were finished, but when I got back to London, we hooked up again and that's when Toby happened." I clear my throat. "After a lot of discussion, Sara decided she'd keep the baby, and we got married. We both tried to make it work and for a while, it did. But then my dad died, and I knew I needed to come back here. The centre was run-down and making a loss, and I was working long hours trying to stop us from going to the wall. Sara was bored and missed her friends, and I guess I wasn't home enough to give her the attention she needed. She started spending more and more time at our flat in London, and then I found out about the jerk she was cheating with."

I glance at Rosie and wonder what she's thinking, but I can't read her expression.

"Sara was here for the weekend, but I could tell she was itching to get back to London. Then it all came out... about her boyfriend and also, she'd decided she was leaving me and Toby. She was prepared to give me sole custody so she could be with him. We had a terrible row before she left." My voice is gruff, my heart pumping hard against my chest, as I relive all the harsh words we'd hurled at each other.

Sara: "Jake doesn't want to be tied down with a child."

Me: "You're Toby's mum - you can't just switch off your responsibilities because it's not convenient with your idiot boyfriend."

Sara: "Yeah, well, you don't have a say in what I do anymore. I want to be with Jake."

Me: "Then be with him. But don't you dare reject Toby. He's done nothing to deserve this. Please, I'm begging you."

Sara: "Jake doesn't like kids. He doesn't want any distractions."

Me: "Toby's not a fucking distraction. He's your son – our son."

Sara: "I'm sorry, but Toby will manage perfectly fine with you. Jake and I want to be together, and Toby will just make things more difficult."

Me: "Make things more difficult...what the hell does that even mean?"

We'd both yelled at each other for an interminable amount of time and then Sara had left. I'd stood on the drive holding Toby in my arms and watched as she'd driven away without a backward glance.

"That was the last time I saw her. The police said she was 3 times over the legal limit when she crashed her car." I run out of words; there's nothing left to say. I feel like I've been in a priest's confessional but without the longed-for absolution. There'll never be absolution, because I can't forgive myself or Sara for wrecking Toby's life. "The guilt eats me up every day." A crushing weight of regret steals my breath, and my voice breaks.

Rosie reaches out and pulls me in for a hug. I let myself relax into her, leaning my forehead gently against hers and closing my eyes. Her heart beats steadily and reassuringly through her summer top, and I breathe in her inner strength like a man starved of oxygen.

There are so many 'what ifs' eating me up inside. What if I'd paid more attention to Sara and less on getting the centre back on its feet? What if we hadn't hurled insults at each other during our last argument, cutting each other to shreds with our anger and resentment? What if Sara hadn't stopped on her way to London and necked the best part of a bottle of vodka before getting back behind the wheel of her car? What if I'd been a better man…a better husband? I could go on and on.

Rosie's body presses up against my chest and her warmth soothes my inner turmoil. She gently rubs her fingertips in circles over my back, and slowly my shaky breathing returns to normal and, after a minute, I pull away.

The only people who know what really happened are Harry and Mrs B. Harry was the one who'd sat with me night after night while I'd drank myself into oblivion over Sara's death. For months I'd wallowed in self-pity while he'd quietly taken over the running of the centre.

Then Mrs B had appeared one morning with a pot of soup. As I was clearly incapable of taking care of Toby and running the house, she'd taken over. I'd been hell-bent on the road to destruction, but gradually Harry and Mrs B had made me realise I needed to keep living for Toby's sake, if not my own. That overriding belief had kept me going in the intervening years.

A dull ache fists my stomach, and I scrape my hands through my hair, trying to make sense of the last few minutes. I don't know why I'd shared all that stuff about Sara. The humiliation of trying to convince Sara to love me and Toby and the agony of her rejection - I'd lain bare my innermost feelings, and I don't even know Rosie. She's not a friend - she's Toby's nanny.

Rosie's perfume lingers in the air, and I breathe it in. It smells of summer; florally and light and it suits her. It occurs to me that I know nothing about Rosie except what's written on her C.V., which isn't anything much. She'd arrived late for her interview and won Toby's affection with her funny sketches. Since then, she's proven a natural with him, their effervescent laughter constantly reverberating throughout the house. Toby's happier than he's ever been, and that's all down to Rosie and her innate way of making everything fun, even when he's helping her with the most mundane of tasks like putting away his toys or making lunch. I'd intended to ask more about her background, but she'd settled into our lives so seamlessly, somehow it had slipped my mind. I realise now that she never talks about her family or her past and I wonder why, and what her story is.

Chapter 10 – Rosie

Happily ever after is a fairy tale…

According to Matt, horse riding makes you happy and relaxed, not to mention the 'special bond' between horse and rider that he assures me is a 'thing'. Yeah, well, I beg to differ! I mean, there's the fear of falling off the damn thing for a start. I'm balanced precariously and then the horse suddenly starts moving, while I'm still trying to figure out how to remain atop the saddle which, by the way, seems a very long way up from the safety of terra firma.

Then there's the sore bum aspect. Having finally made it in one piece to our destination and dismounted, which I have to say I feel pretty proud of mastering, my tender derriere is seriously complaining. On the positive side, it explains why Matt's glutes are so tight and gorgeous because of all the horse riding he does.

Once we've dismounted, we find a place to sit on the grass, and we both gaze down at the scattered Cotswold cottages in the distance. The sun casts dapple-like patterns from the leaves of the trees behind us and Matt turns his face skywards as if he's trying to draw in the heat from the warm day. It's peaceful here, and I shrug off my riding anxiety and slowly relax my tense muscles.

After a while, I tell Matt about Toby and my visit to the churchyard to see Sara. I'm not sure whether he'll be happy about it or not – I'd hate to intrude on their private family grief – but Toby was insistent, so I hope he understands. Then, without thinking, I blurt out, "I can't imagine how awful it must have been when she died."

Matt looks over at me and I'm certain he's going to tell me to mind my own business. But then he seems to change his mind and hesitantly begins reliving his memories of Sara. I'm shocked. I had no idea of the circumstances of her death, but his pain is palpable as he speaks about her. At the end, his voice breaks and, without thinking, I pull him into the safe protection of my arms and hug him like I would Toby if he was hurting. He leans into me, letting me hold his body gently like fragile glass, and we stay like that until he shifts position, and I take it as my cue to release him. He leans back onto his strong arms, his long legs stretched out in front of him, and he clears his throat, resetting the mood.

"So, I've told you the story of my life. What about yours?" Matt looks at me questioningly.

"There's nothing to tell really," I say carefully, though that's a lie and Matt's just opened up to me, so maybe I should do the same about my own loss. I'm actually tempted to, which surprises me. I'm not used to sharing my feelings, though that's probably because nobody outside my family has ever been remotely interested in my life before. But then I dismiss the thought. He's just being polite - after all, I'm just the nanny. Anyway, there's been enough angst for one day.

"No ex-husband or boyfriend?" Matt grins.

"No, definitely neither of those." I laugh. "I've only had one boyfriend, and that was in my last year of school."

"How long were you together?"

"About a year. We'd planned to go to the same university but then my mum got ill, so I stayed at home to look after her."

"I see, hence the many part-time jobs?"

"Yeah, I worked when I could, but mum often needed me at home when she was sick."

"It must have been hard giving up your place at university." His voice is gentle.

"I was sad not to go, but I don't regret it. Mum and I were very close, and it was a privilege to nurse her, and I did it gladly. She died a year ago and then, after everything was dealt with, I got the job in Cornwall."

"With the guy who couldn't keep his hands to himself?"

I look over at him as he puts two and two together. "Yeah."

"You should report him to the agency."

"What would be the point? He'd only deny it and it'd be my word against his."

"Maybe, but at least it would flag it up, especially if he does it again."

"I suppose you're right." I make a mental note to ring the agency, though doubt what good it'll do.

"What happened to the boyfriend?"

"Stu met someone else at university. He's married now."

"I'm sorry." Matt's forehead creases, concern etched in his eyes.

"I'm not. He wasn't nice to me." I pause, remembering. Mum was dying. I knew this because she'd sat me down one day after school and told me. She'd explained it in the calm matter-of-fact way she always had and that she'd already put her affairs in order, so I didn't need to worry when the time came.

I was already familiar with heart-breaking grief, but now the certainty of losing mum was too hard to bear. I was bitterly unhappy at the unfairness but, instead of supporting me to cope with the enormity of mum's illness, Stu had exploited my sadness and misery with his abusive, bullying ways.

We'd met when he'd joined the school in my last year. He was the opposite of me – the cool, confident, sporty one all the girls wanted to go out with. And I was the shy book nerd nobody wanted to go out with. Except he did, and I thought he genuinely liked me. But in the end, it felt more like he despised me, and it shattered every ounce of my self-esteem. He'd hurt me badly and maybe that was why I hadn't dated much since.

"I've never been in love, but I'd like to think that one day I'll fall head over heels and live happily ever after." I can't help smiling at my clichéd statement. "What about you?" I turn the tables. "I hear you have a girlfriend. It's good you're moving on."

"Belle and I aren't serious."

A little jumping bean of joy leaps about inside me at his words. "So, what are you - friends with benefits?" I grin mischievously.

Matt clears his throat. "Blimey, Rosie, who uses terms like that."

"Sorry, it's none of my business." I hold up my palms in apology. Even so, I can't help speculating about his relationship with Belle and what type of woman he finds attractive. No doubt she shares his love of horses and, of course, she'd have to adore Toby. I mean, that's a given, right? But then I remember Caz saying Belle wasn't the maternal type, so maybe he's not serious about her, because he'd like Toby to have a brother or sister one day. Or he's still not over Sara. Actually, scrub that thought. It's abundantly clear he's not over Sara.

"What I mean is, unlike you, I think 'happily ever after' is a fairy tale." Matt's eyes look at mine steadily.

I shake my head because I'm sure he's wrong. My mind fills with my own heart-breaking loss. Loss I've gradually come to terms with, in part, because I do wholeheartedly believe in the possibility of 'happily ever after' though not in a twee fairy tale way. More that, by accepting the devastating events of my past, I've finally found the courage to face my future even though the people I've loved most in the world won't be there to share it with me.

"Well, I'm sure you'll find the love of your life and so will I."

"No, I'm done with relationships." Matt's voice is firm, his dark eyes suddenly clouding over. It's obvious our easy connection from earlier has ended; his concrete walls are back up again, his emotions closed and impenetrable. He suddenly glances at his watch. "We'd better get back – it won't be long until Toby's out of school."

He rises to his feet and starts walking towards the grazing horses, leaving me staring after him, an intense knot of emotion swirling inside me I can't decipher. I know he's hurting, though, and now I know why.

Chapter 11 – Matt

I was young and naïve…

I still don't know why I'd told Rosie about Sara. I usually keep my emotions buried deep inside me, squashed down hard so they never escape. But, for some reason, I'd let Rosie in and the words had spilled out of me, leaving a black oil slick of self-loathing in their wake. I'd expected judgement; blame even, but she'd simply hugged me as I'd tried to hold myself together.

Afterwards, for a few precious moments, I'd felt a fragile sense of peace, and even that one day I'd move past the futility of her death and remember the Sara I first knew. A bright, beautiful, feisty girl who'd captured my heart at university. We'd been happy for a while, and maybe we should never have got back together, but then Toby wouldn't have been born, and I could never ever regret that.

My chest tightens as I remember how much optimism I'd felt at the start of our marriage. I knew Sara was reluctant to have our baby, but I was filled with confidence that once he was born, she'd love him just as much as me. Maybe because I was so desperate for that to happen, I blocked out all my niggling doubts. I believed I had enough love for both of us and that we'd build a future together. I was young and naïve… and I was wrong.

I'll always live with a huge juggernaut of guilt inside me, that I couldn't make our marriage work and I repeat the promise I made to myself after Sara died that I'll never trust my heart to fall in love again. Rosie might believe in 'happily ever after' but she hasn't had her world crash down around her in a million pieces, too hard to ever mend.

Chapter 12 – Rosie

School couldn't teach me, so maybe I'm a lost cause…

Janine and I are meeting up after we've dropped the boys at school, and I'm going to repeat my offer to help her improve her reading and writing. I've already done a little research and found out that the local adult education centre runs English classes and offers a range of qualifications. The library also has family learning classes which support parents to get more involved in their children's learning.

I know from my brother's experience that dyslexia can be a barrier to learning, but he was fortunate that a patient teacher at his school took the time to help him. That isn't always the case, though. Sometimes learning difficulties are missed and the right support isn't put in place, and that might be what's happened to Janine. In any event, I'm glad she's confided in me, and I'll do whatever I can to help her.

We're sitting at her kitchen table drinking tea when I broach the subject and show her the adult education website on my phone, with the range of English classes available.

"They'll do an assessment, which is just a way of finding out what you know already and the things they can help you with. Imagine learning is like a brick wall; there may be some bricks missing at the base of the wall and these are the gaps in your learning. Your tutor will find out what those gaps are and then design a learning plan so that the bricks or gaps get filled in."

"I suppose that makes sense. I just feel so embarrassed, and I don't know if I have the courage to go along to a class. What if everyone else is better than me?"

"Honestly, I think everyone in the class will be in the same boat as you. They're all there because they want to get better at English and the tutors are especially trained to teach adults, so it's not like school at all."

"I don't know – I'll think about it. I mean, school couldn't teach me, so maybe I'm a lost cause."

"You're definitely not a lost cause. I know in my brother's case, he needed a different approach to learning, and he could get extra time in exams because of his dyslexia. Why don't you give them a chance? I'll come with you for the initial assessment if you like?"

"You'd do that for me?" Janine stares at me and I sense she's wavering, so I give her a final push.

"Of course, why don't we ring up the adult education centre now and make an appointment?" Janine nods, and I grab my phone before she changes her mind.

After a few moments, Janine speaks to a friendly manager who explains there's a choice of English classes available during the day or in the evening. Once the assessment has been done, they will offer her a suitable class to attend. The class is for 2.5 hours once a week and there will also be homework. Alternatively, she can do the class online if she prefers. By a stroke of luck, after consulting her appointments diary, there's a time slot available for the assessment this afternoon so Janine agrees to be at the centre at 1 p.m.

"I can't believe I've done that." Janine puts the phone down and smiles at me.

"How do you feel?"

"I feel really proud of myself – like I've done something really brave."

"Well, you have, and that's just the beginning. Just imagine how good you'll feel once you start the class."

***

The adult education centre is situated inside an old building in the centre of town. The place looks run down and in need of refurbishment, with paint peeling off the walls and a general air of having seen better days. However, the receptionist greets us with a reassuring smile, and the atmosphere is warm and welcoming, which is just as well because Janine looks terrified.

After a few moments, we're introduced to a tutor called Anne. She's probably in her late 40s with dark brown hair tied into a ponytail and friendly eyes that crinkle at the edges like she's used to laughing. After introductions, we're both taken into a small side room off reception and Anne explains about the class and what's going to happen next.

"The entire purpose of the class is to help you achieve your goals, whether that's a qualification or just to gain confidence with English. When you've finished your assessment, I'll go through it with you and explain anything you don't understand. We're a friendly bunch and I'm sure you'll soon make friends. Everyone's here to get better at English so they can help their children or maybe get a job or a promotion. You'll find everyone tries to support each other.

"The first thing I'm going to ask is that you do a piece of writing. You can write about anything you like but to give you some ideas, you might write about your family or maybe a holiday you've been on or a hobby that you enjoy. It's always easier to write about something you know."

Janine settles down to her task and after she's finished writing, the tutor gives her some feedback.

"I really enjoyed reading about Olly." Anne smiles kindly at Janine. "He sounds a lovely little boy. There are a few spelling and punctuation mistakes, and we'll work on paragraphs which will make your writing easier to read." She goes through everything in a bit more detail and Janine listens carefully. "There are spaces in a class on a Tuesday morning at 10 a.m. You could take Olly to school and then come along to the class after that."

"That would be great, but how much will all this cost?" Janine asks quietly, biting down on her bottom lip.

"Oh, my dear, the class is free and so are the qualifications. The only things you'll need are an A4 lined notebook and a pen. You might also want to buy a folder so you can keep your work tidy."

"I can't believe it's free!" Janine looks at her in amazement.

"Well, I think that's everything unless you've got any more questions? Shall I see you tomorrow at 10?"

"Thank you, thank you." Janine almost hugs Anne, a grin growing broader across her face.

"You're very welcome. We're here to help you and if you ever have any concerns or worries about the class, please come and talk to me."

"I'm sure I won't. Now I've met you, I feel so much better."

***

As we're leaving the centre, we notice a small community café attached to the side of the building. It looks inviting, with red and white gingham tablecloths and bright, modern artwork displayed on the whitewashed walls. And when we go inside, the smell of coffee and freshly baked bread greets us. It's a popular place with most tables occupied, but as we're scanning the room for an empty table, we notice Caz sitting by the window, so we go over to join her.

"You'll never guess what I've done!" Janine exclaims, her excitement bubbling to the surface.

"No, I don't think I will, so you'd better tell me." Caz laughs.

While Janine is filling Caz in on her eventful day, I go to the counter to buy the drinks and treat us to some cake too, as it's turning into a bit of a celebration. When the drinks arrive, Caz and I toast Janine with our mugs of strong builders' tea.

"Here's to your new class and your success."

While we sit chatting and eating cake, Caz notices me looking around at the young servers in the café and explains.

"The café is run as a 'not for profit' business for the benefit of the catering students. They learn all kinds of kitchen and waiting skills which will help them find work in a restaurant when they finish their course. I always come here when I'm in town; the cakes are delicious, and it's a good way of supporting the centre too."

We chat some more, enjoying the relaxed, sociable atmosphere in the café. Then, mindful that the boys will soon be out of school, say our goodbyes to Caz and get up to leave.

"I just remembered... it's quiz night at the pub tomorrow." Caz catches my arm. "Why don't you ask Matt for the night off and come along? It starts at 8 o'clock, and it's a good laugh."

"That sounds fun. I'll definitely ask him and let you know."

We arrive at school a few minutes before the boys are due to come out. It's been a busy day, but I feel optimistic that this is the start of something positive for Janine.

Chapter 13 – Rosie

I love it when he smiles…

Matt's agreed to my night off and, after Toby's in bed, I quickly change and put make-up on. My usual look's minimal – a touch of mascara and lip-gloss - but I decide to make more effort and apply smoky grey eye shadow and pink lipstick, which complement my pink top and best jeans. My work hair is usually tied back in a ponytail or messy bun, but I leave my hair down and, for once, my loose waves behave and look glossy and smooth. After a quick spray of expensive 'save it for a special occasion' perfume, I grab my purse and phone and head downstairs.

Matt's working in the sitting room, and he looks up from his laptop when I go in. "You look lovely." His eyes hold mine.

"Thanks, I'm a little nervous, to be honest."

"Caz will be there and Harry too, I expect. It'll be fine."

"Yeah, I'm sure you're right." *I wish you were coming with me.* "I shouldn't be too late."

"Have fun." His lips turn up slightly into a gentle smile, and his eyes crease at the corners. I love it when he smiles. It's like a rare gift, and when it happens, it smooths out the seriousness he normally wears on his face. It's intoxicating too, making me tipsy and wanting more. Then his gaze returns to his laptop, and it feels like a dismissal. But, as I slowly turn towards the door, his dark eyes fix on me again.

Butterflies are salsa dancing in my tummy, but I'm pretty sure these aren't pub quiz nerves. Heat burns my cheeks, and it takes all my willpower to walk out of the door when all I want to do is turn around and stay home with Matt.

Chapter 14 - Matt

Plump black cherries…

Rosie looks beautiful when she comes downstairs. Her golden hair is loose for a change, falling into soft waves over her shoulders, and I have a sudden desire to run my fingers through its smooth silkiness. She's also wearing more makeup than usual; her full pink lips glossy and kissable. *Jesus - I sound like a sex-starved teenager.* I fist my hands tightly and shove them, along with my improper thoughts, down by my side.

Rosie looks at me nervously, and I do my best to reassure her she'll enjoy the quiz night, though a part of me - the selfish part - wants her to stay home with me. That's not an option though so, while she's still hesitating, I tell her to have fun and return my gaze to my laptop screen. I'm good at that - closing down conversations and making people go away – and that's exactly what Rosie does. She turns and leaves the room, but not before my eyes jerk back up again, so I can follow her retreating back. I want to call out to her;

to make up an excuse and insist she stays. I'm her boss after all, so I could do that but, of course, I don't.

After she's left, I try to do some work, but my mind isn't on it. I can still smell her perfume, and it's making me lose focus. It smells different from her usual one – sexier. It reminds me of plump black cherries – luscious and heady - teasing my senses with unfulfilled fantasies.

Suddenly my mobile goes off, and I grab it from the coffee table and answer on the second ring; worry racing through my head that Rosie's ancient car has broken down. Without checking the name, I blurt out, "Are you okay?"

A silky voice answers at the other end. "Well, that's lovely of you to be so concerned, Matt. I've just had a late business meeting and rather than drive back to London, I wondered if I could crash at yours?"

"Belle, sorry, I thought you were… it doesn't matter. Of course, that's fine. Where are you?"

"I'm at Stow. I should be with you in about half an hour. Sorry it's short notice, but I've missed you so much and now this work project's finished, I thought it would be nice to catch up."

I swallow down the urge to make up an excuse, mainly because I can't think of one instantly off the top of my head, and she takes my silence as consent.

I'd met Belle a year ago at the Cheltenham Festival. I was there on a rare day out with Harry and Caz, and I'd literally bumped into her as we were about to watch the Gold Cup. She was with a group of her posh 'Hooray Henry' friends and, after apologising profusely for nearly knocking her over, we'd watched the race together. Belle's horse, the favourite, won easily, and we'd celebrated with champagne, which flowed extravagantly throughout the sultry afternoon.

I guess I'd been flattered by her blatant play for me. She'd flirted outrageously and I couldn't resist her, not so subtle, invitation to go back to her hotel room. We'd spent the night together but, as far as I was concerned, we weren't likely to see each other again. Then, a few weeks later, Belle got back in touch, and it became a more regular hook-up. An occasional night or weekend together suited us both, without commitment or pressure for anything more.

We haven't seen each other for a few weeks; actually, thinking about it, it's been almost three months, as she's been focusing on building up her interior design business. She's driven, ambitious and single-minded about her career, and finally, all her hard work is paying off, and she's becoming noticed by those who matter in her profession. Her latest commission is featured in a well-respected style magazine, and I'm proud of her growing success and reputation.

Belle's attractive and intelligent, and her sharp humour makes her entertaining company when she's in the right mood. Her fiery nature can be hard work, but, on the other hand, life is never dull when she's around. One reason our occasional hook-ups have worked so far is that I don't get to see her moodier side that often. The saying, 'absence makes the heart grow fonder' is certainly true in Belle's case.

The last time we'd spent the night together, Belle admitted she wanted our casual arrangement to change. Of course, she deserves a more serious relationship, but it can't be with me. I sit in the fading light mulling over what I should do, but in fact, my decision is easy. I need to end things with her and, since she's on her way over, there's no time like the present. I can't pretend I have the ability to love her, or anyone else, for that matter. I lost that the day Sara died.

***

Belle arrives shortly before 10 p.m. and by the number of Gucci cases she has with her, I realise that she's not planning to stay just one night but intends a longer visit. I lead her into the kitchen and brace myself.

"I told you a tiny fib... I'm hoping you'll let me stay a little while longer. My flat's being refurbished, and the builders are running a tad behind. Also, I've really missed you, so I thought we could spend some time together. I'm sorry I've neglected you, but I really want to make it up to you."

Belle's emerald eyes fix on mine. She's a natural redhead and her long claret locks and pale complexion, not to mention her height of nearly 6 foot, make her appearance striking. Tonight, she's wearing a fitted cream trouser suit which looks expensive, and 3-inch heels which bring her almost to my height.

"Belle, we should talk."

"I know I've been a complete bitch to stay away for so long. I had this enormous commission to finish, and I needed to concentrate on that. But now it's done ... I'm all yours darling and I really want to make it up to you."

Her voice is sultry and sexy, and she walks over to where I'm standing and trails her long ruby-red nails over my stubble. Slowly, she places her arms around my neck, pulling me in for a kiss. She knows she looks stunning, but tonight I'm immune to her attempts at seduction.

"Belle," I say, stepping back, "I mean it. We really need to talk."

"Well, okay then, but please, not tonight. I've had a really tiring day, and all I want is a large glass of wine and a long soak in the bath. How about you join me?"

"Look, we'll talk in the morning but–."

"Fine, let's at least enjoy this evening. How about you open the wine while I go change into something more comfortable?"

And before I can say anything more, she winks at me and sashays out of the room while I'm still standing there figuring out how I've got myself into this mess.

***

Belle's an expert at deflection. She chatters on about her latest work project and the nightmare clients who are making her life an 'absolute misery'. Apparently, the enormous fees she charges won't compensate for all the stress and sleepless nights they're causing her.

She's sitting up in bed in the guest room, mimicking their voices in a mocking drawl, her acerbic wit in full flow. I know she's doing her best to amuse me, her black low-cut silk negligee an invitation for me to join her, which I have absolutely no intention of doing. I decide I've had enough of her efforts at distraction. If she won't talk about the subject that's really on both our minds, then I need to get out of here. I make my excuses and go into my bedroom to shower.

I stand under the shower head for a few minutes, letting the hot jets wash over me until the tight knots of tension ease from my body. I should have stopped Belle from coming here tonight. I don't want to hurt her, but our 'no-strings' hook-ups are over and any desire she might have for a more serious relationship isn't happening either. The water soothes me and hardens my resolve. I won't let her deflect anymore. We need to clear the air and the sooner the better.

Suddenly, I hear Toby calling out, his voice hysterical and frightened. I grab some sweatpants and rush into his room. He's sitting up in bed, still half asleep but wide-eyed and panic-stricken. He's clearly in a bad dream. "It's okay, buddy. I'm here."

I reach over and hold him in my arms as he clings to me. He's breathing hard and crying, although he's still not properly awake. I stroke his hair and rub my hand up and down his back to calm him. Gradually his breathing eases, as I continue talking softly to him, and he falls back to sleep again.

After I'm certain he's sleeping soundly, I tiptoe out of his room and, as I emerge onto the landing, I see Rosie coming upstairs. Her eyes wander over my bare chest and her embarrassment is adorable when she realises I've noticed, her cheeks turning a beautiful shade of blush pink. Is it wrong that I like how I'm affecting her? Probably, but my ego doesn't care. After she's recovered her composure and we've exchanged news – me about Toby's nightmare and Rosie about the pub quiz – suddenly Belle's sultry voice calls out.

"Matt, darling."

Damn, did Belle really need to say, darling?

Rosie's like a rabbit caught in headlights; a desperate need in her eyes to rush past me and escape to her room, but I need to tell her… to explain what Belle's doing here before she gets the wrong impression.

"Belle arrived unexpectedly," is all that comes out of my mouth.

"Well, that's nice for you," she replies.

We stare at each and, for the life of me, I can't think of anything else to say. I'm irritated though. No, it's more than that. I'm pissed off with myself that I've allowed the situation with Belle to get out of hand.

Then I step out of the way so Rosie can get past me.

"Night, Rosie." It sounds like a dismissal, but it's all I can manage.

Chapter 15 – Rosie

Matt, darling...

It's nearly midnight when I arrive back at the house, and I notice there's an unfamiliar car parked outside. It's strange Matt hadn't mentioned he was expecting any callers tonight. I open the front door, grateful that the porch and hallway lights are on, so I can see what I'm doing. The house is quiet, and the rest of the downstairs is in darkness, with no sign of Matt or his night-time visitor, as I make my way upstairs.

Just as I reach the top, Matt emerges from Toby's room, blocking the landing and the way to my room. My eyes travel slowly down his bare chest, taking in the light dusting of dark hair that disappears beneath his sweatpants. He's got just the right amount of muscle – not an over-exercised gym body – no, his is just perfect, toned from physical hard work and riding.

Matt leans against Toby's door frame, a wicked smirk forming on his face as he realises I'm staring at him.

"Is everything okay?" I ask once I've dragged my eyes upwards to meet his grinning face. I feel my cheeks colour at being caught blatantly ogling his chest, and I will myself not to let my eyes wander down again, even though I'm tempted.

"Yeah, fine, Toby's had a bad dream."

"Shall I go into him?"

"No, he's asleep again now. How was your evening?"

"Great, we came second. We would have come first if we'd known the state flower of New York." I pout.

His brows furrow. "It's the rose, I think".

"OMG, how did you know that?"

"My sister lived in Manhattan for a bit before moving to Kansas, so I probably got it from her."

"You need to come to the quiz next time – not that I'm competitive or anything."

"Maybe." He laughs and my breath catches because I love its deep, rumbly sound.

Suddenly an insistent voice calls out, "Matt, darling."

There's an awkward moment between us … a beat of silence before Matt tries to speak. But I butt in. "Well, I'd better get to bed - G-night."

Only I can't go anywhere because he's blocking the landing. And if I try to move past him, our bodies will bump into each other.

"Belle arrived unexpectedly." His eyes meet mine and there's something about his expression that I can't quite read. But the easy-going atmosphere has changed.

"Well, that's nice for you."

I wait for him to move out of the way, but he remains where he is. Maybe he wants to say something else, but the silence grows heavier, and I shift from one foot to the other.

Finally, Matt steps aside. "Night, Rosie." His brisk tone is a pinprick, deflating my cheerful mood.

"Night." I skip past him, aware that his eyes are following me as I escape into my room.

***

It's early still, morning sunshine flooding the kitchen through the open patio doors. Matt's already at the stables and I'm sitting at the table sipping my tea, letting my mind drift to last night.

I wasn't expecting Belle to be here when I got back and, by his awkward expression when we'd faced each other across the landing, neither was Matt. In fact, when she'd called out his name, he'd seemed oddly embarrassed - or maybe annoyed - certainly not like a man delighted his girlfriend had turned up for the night. Something was definitely off. Still, whatever's going on is none of my business. I just need to act professionally, and any feelings I've stupidly allowed to surface towards Matt will soon disappear. I heave out an exasperated sigh because I'm pretty sure I'm lying to myself.

"Well, hello there. You must be the new nanny."

I look up from my daydream and see a tall redheaded woman appraising me. She's wearing fitted jeans which highlight her endlessly long, slim legs, and a white cotton shirt, which on me would look ordinary, but on her is effortlessly stylish. Her makeup is subtle and emphasises her beautiful green eyes and pale skin. She must be Belle, and I quickly get up and offer her my hand to shake.

"Hi, yes, I'm Rosie," I say, giving her a friendly smile but noticing that she doesn't return it.

"Well, nanny, I wonder if you would pop into town later and pick up a few things for me."

Her voice is confident and authoritative, and I have the impression that this isn't a request but an instruction. She's talking to me as an employee, which, of course, I am.

"No problem. What would you like me to get?" I look back at her with my smile still firmly in place.

Just then, Matt walks into the kitchen and takes in the scene.

"Oh, I see you two have met." He looks at me and then back at Belle.

"Yes, I was just asking nanny to get me a few essentials after she takes Tobias to school."

Matt raises his eyebrows and then aims a firm look at Belle. "She's not your maid, Belle."

"It's fine," I interject. "Just leave me a list, and I'll get everything you need."

I flee the kitchen on the pretext of waking Toby for breakfast and thankfully, by the time I come back downstairs, Matt and Belle are nowhere to be seen. A sense of relief floods through me, and I concentrate on getting Toby's food and hope we can leave for school before they return.

***

Just as I'm getting Toby into the car, Belle appears at the front door, waving a piece of paper at me. She steps out onto the drive and hands me a neatly written shopping list, most items of which I've never heard of.

"I'm not sure if I'll be able to find all of these, but I'll do my best."

"I'm sure they'll be available in a decent health food store. Oh, and tonight Matt and I will be having a quiet dinner so …"

"Yes, of course. I'll eat with Toby and stay in my room afterwards."

Belle nods and returns to the house. I take a deep, calming breath and look at the list again. I'll definitely need to go into Cheltenham if I stand any chance of finding these unusual (a.k.a weird) items: organic sea moss, goji berries, chia seeds and spirulina anyone? I heave out a sigh. I'd hoped to go over to Janine's today and help her with some homework she has to do for college. Still, with a bit of luck, I'll get Belle's shopping done and I can meet up with Janine later.

***

I drop Toby at the school gate and watch as he skips happily into school with Olly. They look so sweet together, their arms linked as they make their way into the playground. The sound of shrieking and squealing, a high-pitched and excited hullabaloo, fills the air and I stand listening, enjoying the loud din all the children are making. It reminds me of my carefree school days when I had dreams and ambitions for the future before my mum got sick.

I notice Janine walking towards me; her face smiling in greeting, and I quickly shake myself out of my introspection. "I'm sorry, Janine, I know I said I'd help you with your homework this morning, but I need to go into Cheltenham to buy some things for Matt's girlfriend."

"No problem. I can always email my tutor if I get stuck."

"If I get back in time, I'll pop over before school finishes."

"Honestly, Rosie, please don't worry. Anyway, what she like… Matt's girlfriend, I mean?"

I hesitate. I've only just met her and there's not been enough time to form an objective opinion. Even so, it's hard to ignore my instinct that Belle doesn't like me; she's not exactly been friendly towards me. I decide to stick with a simple description rather than an emotional response.

"She's beautiful and elegant; they certainly make a striking couple. She's almost his height."

"Who are you talking about?" Caz appears at our side. I notice that the purple streaks in her hair have changed to a lighter pink, and she's wearing a bright candy pink coat, the colour of seaside rock.

"Matt's girlfriend." Janine winks. "She's got Rosie running errands already."

Caz raises her eyebrows. "Really?"

"Oh, just a few bits she needs. Anyway, I'd better fly."

I leave them both at the school gate and head back to my car, looking down at the long list of health foods on the list and wondering where to start with tracking them all down.

Chapter 16 – Rosie

An eccentric old lady who has lots of cats…

Belle's shopping list has led me on a merry dance, and I've spent several hours hunting down ingredients to make what I gather are superfood shakes. Despite the helpful assistants in the specialist health food shops I've visited, I'm still a couple of items short and I've ordered these so I can collect them tomorrow. I'm pleased with my morning's endeavours, and there's also still time to pop in to see Janine before I pick Toby up from school.

Janine's looking pleased with herself too as she's completed her homework tasks, and we both celebrate our successful day with mugs of tea and chocolate biscuits.

"I have news." Janine looks at me, smiling. "I have a date… well, it's not exactly a date. We're just going out for a coffee, but still."

"Whoa, you're going on a date – that's brilliant."

"Yeah, I know. First date I've had in … well, forever. He's at college too but doing maths. Anyway, it's only a coffee, but you never know."

"What's his name?"

"It's Liam. He works for Matt at the stables." Janine's eyes are shining with excitement.

"Oh, I know Liam. I met him at the riding centre, and he was at the quiz last night. He seems nice."

It's obvious that Janine's a little love-struck and we're still chatting about her upcoming date while we walk the short distance to the school to collect the boys.

"If the coffee date goes well, and he asks you out one evening, then Olly can come to ours for a sleepover if you'd like. It'll give you a bit more privacy."

"You mean I can have wild rampant sex without Olly interrupting us." Janine laughs, and her cheeks colour up at the thought.

"Well, you never know your luck," I tease.

"What about you… anyone you've got your eye on?"

"I wish. No, I'm destined to become an eccentric old lady who has lots of cats. Isn't there a funny poem about growing old? Something about wearing purple and eating sausages…can't remember the whole thing, but that's definitely going to be me."

"Don't be daft." Janine hugs me. "It's a pity Matt's got a girlfriend. I think you'd be great together."

"No, I'm better off with lots of cats and sausages!"

***

I feel like I've been summoned to the head teacher's study, and I'm about to be given detention. It might be funny if my legs weren't actually shaking.

"I'm sorry, Belle, I couldn't get all the items on your shopping list, but I've ordered them, and I'll pick them up tomorrow."

"Well, I suppose living in a backwater, it's to be expected. Just make sure you get the rest of the things tomorrow."

I nod in agreement, feeling relief that she's taken it so well, and sidle towards the door of Matt's study where she's been working at his desk.

"Just a moment, tell me, what childcare qualifications do you have?" Belle's cool green eyes appraise me.

"Uh, well… I don't have any, but Matt knows that."

"Oh, I see." Belle draws out the words, emphasising each one, and continues to study me. "I would have thought professional training was essential. After all, you're looking after a young vulnerable child grieving his mother. Are you experienced in childhood trauma?"

"I… I hadn't really considered…" I mumble, but Belle cuts me off.

"You have an enormous responsibility towards Tobias. I'm quite surprised Matt employed you… he can be too altruistic sometimes."

Her words jolt me, but then I wonder if she's right. Toby's had so much loss in his short life, and I'd hate to let Matt down by being incompetent at my job. And perhaps he only hired me because he felt sorry for me. I stand miserably as self-doubt takes root in my head, but when I look up,

Belle's focus is no longer on me but back on her laptop screen.

Chapter 17 – Matt

Who's Rolly?

I've been at the Equestrian centre all day, dealing with a mare with colic, a potential new client who wants to place her two horses in full livery, and a disgruntled woman complaining about her 'uncooperative' horse during a riding lesson. Of course, it had to be the horse's fault rather than her clear lack of horsemanship skill.

Belle's also been on my mind all day. I'd intended to talk to her first thing this morning, but I'd been called away at dawn because the vet was urgently needed for the colic case. It's nearly 5 p.m. as I make my way back to the house. Toby will be home from school, and hopefully, I'll be able to clear the air with Belle this evening.

In the kitchen, there's a hive of activity going on. Toby and Rosie are sitting at the kitchen table engrossed in creating something, though I'm not exactly sure what. There's an array of clean yogurt pots, cardboard loo roll holders, different sized coloured buttons, pasta shapes, pipe cleaners and small stickers lying on the table.

"Whatcha making, son?" I sit down next to him and ruffle his hair as I watch him concentrating on sticking bits of pipe cleaner onto a yogurt pot.

Toby looks up from what he's doing. "It's a robot. Look, the yogurt pot's the body, and the pipe cleaners are the arms. I'm going to use another small pot for its head and stick buttons on to make its eyes and mouth."

"It looks great." I kiss the top of his head and look over at what Rosie's doing.

"And what are you making?"

"I'm making a brother for Rolly."

"Who's Rolly?"

"Rolly – you know – Rolly the Robot!" She winks at me.

"Ah, I see, and what's your robot called?" I grin.

"Jeff." Her lips crease into a big smirk.

"Jeff?" I raise my eyebrows.

"Yep, Jeff - brother of Rolly!" Rosie's sparkling eyes are full of laughter.

"Wow, well then, maybe I can make a sister for Rolly and Jeff." I wink back at her, and we both burst out laughing just as Belle comes into the kitchen.

"Hi, Belle," I say as I try to stop myself from laughing. "Do you fancy making a robot?"

Abruptly, Rosie pushes up from her chair. "Sorry, I meant to be a lot more organised with tea. I'll get this all cleared up, so Toby and I can eat."

"No, it's fine. Let's finish the robots, and we can all eat in a while." I give her a reassuring smile as I grab a couple of cardboard loo roll holders and a yogurt pot.

Belle stands by the table, looking between Rosie and me, before her green eyes capture mine. "I thought I could make a special dinner for just the two of us.... It'll give us the chance to talk."

Rosie's slowly moving away from the table, but I'll be damned if I'm going to break off the fun.

"How about we finish the robots and then you and I can go to the pub for something to eat?" I hold my breath, wondering if she'll argue.

"Okay then." Belle smiles sweetly back at me and I let out the breath I've been holding in, patting the chair next to me. She walks over to me and grazes my lips with a slow, sensuous kiss, and runs her long fingernails through my hair. I pull away clumsily, feeling awkward, but when I look up, Rosie's no longer in the room.

Chapter 18 - Rosie

It's the Matt effect…

Toby loves drawing, painting and making things. I've collected enough recycled materials to create funny little robots out of yogurt pots and bits and bobs, which I know he'll adore doing. I'd planned an hour or so of this and then a quick tea before Toby and I disappear upstairs for bath time, leaving Belle and Matt to their romantic evening.

We're in the middle of lots of creativity and sticky mess when Matt arrives home. He's soon joining in though, and his teasing laughter at my choice of robot names evaporates all the tension clinging to me from my earlier run-in with Belle. It's the Matt effect - a topsy-turvy sensation that tangles up my insides - making me feel buoyant and giddy with happiness because he's making silly robots with Toby and me.

There's no time to think about that though because Belle comes into the kitchen, and I notice the time. It's much later than I'd realised, and I jump up quickly so I can start making tea for Toby and me. But Matt has other ideas.

"Let's finish the robots and we can all eat in a while."

He gives me a reassuring smile, but I only have to look at Belle's body language to know she's cross with me. While Matt's trying to placate her about the intimate meal for two she'd planned, I take the chance to escape the kitchen because I badly need to regain my composure. Every instinct I have tells me that Belle doesn't want me here at all, and I wonder if she'll try to persuade Matt to let me go. I'm still on trial so... A heavy dread settles in the pit of my stomach at that thought.

***

I sit on the edge of my bed, waiting for my heartbeat to slow down. If Matt changes his mind and fires me, I'll be back to square one again – without a job or a home. Unexpected tears pool in my eyes, blurring my vision. Even though I've only been here a short time, I can't bear the thought of leaving Toby. He's stolen my heart and, as silly as it sounds, I feel I belong here. I felt it the moment I arrived and to leave now would be devastating. My shoulders slump as I try to steady my shaky breathing when there's a knock on my door.

Matt's standing outside, his brows furrowed in worry. "I'm just checking you're okay?"

There's a lump in my throat that I try to swallow down. I nod, but I can't form any words. Perhaps Matt realises, because he carries on speaking softly.

"I really wasn't expecting Belle last night."

"It's your home, Matt. You can invite whoever you want to stay." My voice sounds strange; too high-pitched and sharp.

"I know, but you live here too, and I don't want you to feel uncomfortable." He continues regarding me.

"Well thanks, but I don't," I reply firmly, pulling my professional mask in place and mustering up a confident smile that I don't feel. "I just need to… to… I'll be down in a minute." My words hang in the air between us like a miserable grey day.

"I'll see you downstairs then," Matt replies gently, as I go to close the door.

Chapter 19 – Matt

It was never supposed to get serious…

"Well, this isn't exactly what I'd planned. Still, it's probably better food than I can cook." Belle leans across the table, smiling, her tongue caressing her lips sensuously.

The restaurant's dimly lit, and our table is in a quiet, intimate corner. There's a low hum of conversation from the other diners around us, like whispered secrets floating in the air. Belle's black dress clings to her curves and exposes her bare, milky white shoulders, and her red hair falls naturally in soft waves down her back. She looks alluring and glamorous but completely out of place in this country pub restaurant, where most people are more casually dressed.

"I'm starving. I think I'm going to break all my rules and have something unhealthy and bad for me. Maybe a burger and fries – what about you?" she asks.

We both order burgers with all the toppings together with drinks and, while we're waiting for our food, Belle tries her best to be entertaining and amusing. I feel like a jerk. She's sexy and attractive, and most men would give their right arm to be in her company, but I really don't want to be here.

"How's Rosie getting on? It must be quite a challenge looking after Tobias; he's so full of energy."

"She's doing great, and Toby loves her." I sip my drink, wondering where she's going with this conversation.

"That may be so, darling, but she's not exactly an expert at dealing with his terrible grief over losing his mother? I mean, shouldn't you have a trained person… someone professionally qualified?"

"Toby's doing fine and if I ever have any concerns, of course, I'll arrange whatever support he needs. But Rosie's doing a great job. I mean, you saw how much fun he was having making robots. Rosie's always coming up with fun stuff for him to do."

"I'm just saying that I think you need someone more au fait with childhood trauma. Rosie's nice and all that, but I'm sure you could find someone more… suitable."

"Well, it's kind of you to be concerned, but I'm happy with things the way they are. The last nanny took off with her boyfriend without giving notice. Rosie's reliable and conscientious and, like I said, Toby worships her, which is the most important thing."

Thankfully, our food arrives and the subject's dropped. The burgers are mouth-wateringly delicious, but Belle moves her food around her plate, clearly more used to gourmet delicacies in overpriced London restaurants.

Just then, I see Harry and Caz coming into the restaurant. Harry spots me straight away and walks over with a big grin on his face as I rise from my seat. He embraces me in his usual bear hug, and then holds out his hand to Belle.

"Hi Belle, great to see you. Are you here for long?"

Dammit, I didn't want Harry to ask that.

"I... I don't know Harry. I'm hoping so, but I guess it depends on Matt." She directs her emerald eyes at me, but, thankfully, Caz comes over to join us before I can say anything.

"Hi both... umm, those burgers look amazing. Come on, Harry. Let's leave them to their meal. Maybe catch you later for a drink?"

Normally, I'd ask them to join us, but I need to talk to Belle, and I can't bear the thought of postponing it any longer.

"I definitely recommend the burgers." I smile at Caz but avoid answering about meeting up for a drink. I don't think either of us will be in the mood after our talk.

***

"Do you want to see the dessert menu?" The waitress asks us once our plates have been cleared.

I know Belle won't order anything – I've never seen her eat anything the slightest bit sweet and indulgent, but the waitress waits politely while she leisurely scans the dessert menu before declining.

"No, I'm absolutely stuffed."

"Coffee then, or another drink?" The waitress isn't going to give up.

"A decaffeinated coffee would be good."

I order an espresso. I need all the caffeine I can get.

When our drinks arrive, I take a sip of the strong dark liquid, letting the bitterness hit the back of my throat, and then I put my cup down carefully.

"Belle, we need to talk properly."

"I know what you're going to say." Her green eyes lock onto mine.

"I've never lied to you about this just being a bit of fun between us. It was never supposed to get serious." I stare steadily back at her.

"We're good together, Matt." She reaches for my arm, and I notice that her long nails are perfectly manicured. Everything about Belle is styled and expensive, and for some reason, that irritates me.

"You deserve someone better than me — someone not broken. I can't give you the relationship you want or deserve."

She gives me a long, sultry look through her dark eyelashes. "Please, Matt, I know you're not over Sara yet, but I'll wait until you are."

"I'm sorry." I make my voice sound strong. "I should never have let this thing between us go on for so long – and that's on me - and I'm sorry if I've hurt you or you thought–."

"At least let me stay until the builders finish at my flat this weekend. I promise I'll leave after that, if I haven't persuaded you to change your mind." Her voice is low and seductive as she trails her painted fingernails across my jaw.

This is going to be more difficult than I'd thought. I exhale a deep sigh, and her eyes continue to implore me until I finally give in, as she probably knew I would.

Chapter 20 – Rosie

All sugar and spice…

I move stealthily downstairs, hoping I can avoid bumping into Belle. It's still early and with a bit of luck Toby and I can leave for school before she gets up. I walk into the kitchen and am surprised to see Matt standing at the coffee machine – he's usually at the stables by now. He smiles at me a good morning and hands me a cup of disgusting brown liquid that's masquerading as a drink.

I wonder for the umpteenth time whether I should tell him I don't like coffee, but instead I smile my thanks and, to make it at least palatable, I stir in a heap of sugar.

"Your dentist would be horrified." Matt grins at me.

"Oh well, you know me – all sugar and spice and all that's nice." I laugh, although it's not that funny. "I–umm–I thought you'd be at the stables by now."

"I'm waiting for Belle. We're going riding together." He turns back to the coffee machine, presumably to make his own horrible drink.

"Oh, that's nice." I take a tentative sip of my coffee and decide no amount of sugar will make it pleasant.

Just then, Belle comes into the kitchen. She's wearing riding clothes and, as much as I hate to admit it, Matt and she make the perfect-looking couple standing side by side at the coffee machine. Belle's only a little shorter than Matt – she's model like and statuesque, and today her stunning red hair is up in a stylish bun. In contrast, I'm wearing denim shorts and a faded vintage Abba T-shirt which has seen better days but is one of my favourites. My hair's badly in need of a wash too, so I've pulled it back into an unkempt ponytail. I can't help sighing inwardly at the contrast between us.

"Good morning, nanny, please don't forget to collect the rest of my order today." Belle focuses her green eyes on mine.

"No problem." I smile back at her even though it feels odd to be addressed as 'nanny' because everyone else calls me Rosie.

Matt's still got his back to me, and Belle whispers something close to his ear and drapes her arm over his shoulder, letting her fingers caress where his dark hair curls into his neck. It feels an intimate moment between them – one I shouldn't be witnessing. I leave my barely touched coffee on the kitchen table and make my excuses to go upstairs and wake Toby up for school.

Chapter 21 – Matt

Stop being such an appalling snob…

"You really are a piece of work," I admonish Belle as soon as Rosie's left the room. "What's with the 'nanny' title? Why don't you call her Rosie like everyone else?"

"Well, that's your problem, Matt. If you're over familiar with staff, they'll soon start taking liberties."

"Oh, stop being such an appalling snob. And stop ordering Rosie about like she's your personal assistant."

"I didn't." She looks at me, her green eyes glinting. "I simply reminded her to collect the items she failed to get yesterday."

"She's not even your employee," I fire back at her.

I inhale a deep breath, trying to keep my temper in check. I'm irritated, but there's absolutely no point trying to reason with her when she's in this sort of mood. Then I notice the untouched coffee on the table and realise that Rosie's probably left the kitchen because she's uncomfortable.

There's an atmosphere as soon as they're both in the same room. I felt it yesterday too, and I hate the thought that Rosie feels awkward in her own home. Still, Belle's leaving in a few days and then everything will return to normal again.

"Come on," I order. "Let's go up to the stables now. We'll grab a coffee there."

Chapter 22 – Rosie

Like two Olympic champions…

I'm hiding furtively behind the bedroom curtains in Toby's room while he's getting dressed. I have a good view of the driveway up to the stables and, while I'm half listening to Toby's chatter, I'm carefully observing Matt and Belle as they walk along together. I don't expect Matt will need to find an old 'granny' horse for her. I imagine she's an expert rider already, and they'll be like two Olympic champions as they gallop over the – well, whatever the horsey term is for fields – or maybe there isn't one. Whatever, she'll be a proficient rider, and Matt will tell her how relieved he is that she doesn't need instruction on how to mount a horse and how boring it was taking me out riding the other day.

Stop it! I tell myself off firmly. Belle's Matt's girlfriend, and instead of spying on them, I need to liven up my own life – maybe a girl's night out with plenty of wine, gossip and a good laugh would do the trick. I wonder if Caz and

Janine are free and I quickly message them both, hoping we can arrange something soon.
***

I'm in big trouble. The items I've ordered for Belle haven't arrived and won't be available until the weekend. I've popped back home before I collect Toby from school, and I just hope she takes the news better than I think. I brace myself as I knock on Matt's office door to break the bad news.

Belle's sitting behind Matt's desk, concentrating on her laptop screen. She doesn't look up and I hover at the entrance to the room, unsure whether I should go in. She's changed her riding clothes, and she looks elegant and chic in a jade green silk dress, every bit the successful businesswoman. I briefly wonder where Matt is, though I doubt he can save me from my fate.

I clear my throat, hoping she'll look up. "Umm…Belle, I'm afraid–"

"One moment," she commands, pointing her index finger in the air, but she still doesn't look up. She's clearly concentrating on something important.

I shift from one foot to the other, uncomfortably aware that in a moment or two she's going to give me a piercing look of disappointment, although I might count myself lucky if that's all that happens. The clock on the wall ticks ominously. I've never been aware of the clock before, but now it's all I can concentrate on. The ticking sound cuts through the silence and reverberates around the room.

"Well?" She finally looks at me, her eyes questioning.

"I…" The roof of my mouth is dry and my words tangle, so I swallow and try again. "I'm afraid the order hasn't arrived. They say it'll be Saturday now."

"What – that's ridiculous. Where did you order them from…some backstreet discount place?"

"No, I ordered them from the big health food shop in Cheltenham, but they say they're difficult to get hold of."

"Absolute nonsense." Her lips set in a tight line, and her eyes stab me like darts on a board.

Suddenly, I'm aware of the door to the office opening, and Matt walks in. He looks between us both, taking in the scene, his eyebrows furrowing. "What's happened?"

"I was just telling Belle…"

"You may go, nanny." She glares at me.

Maybe Matt realises I desperately want to escape, because he jerks his head towards the door. "You go, Rosie." He smiles at me, but I'm too upset to smile back. I turn tail as quickly as I can and bolt up to my room.

***

I stand in the ensuite in my bedroom and splash cold water onto my face, trying to slow down my breathing from its "fight or flight" reaction. What's wrong with me? I need to get a grip and stop allowing Belle to intimidate me. Suddenly, my phone pings loudly with an incoming message. I grab a hand towel to dry my face and pick my phone up from the bedside table.

Caz: Great idea about a night out – how about TONIGHT???

Caz: I know it's short notice, but Janine can get a babysitter!
Caz: And Harry's offered to be our taxi driver!
Me: I'll have to check with Matt, but sounds great.
Me: And big hugs to Harry – he's the best!!!

Just then there's a gentle tap on my door and when I open it, Matt's standing outside.

"I just want to check you're okay?" His intelligent eyes study my face.

"This is becoming a habit." I grin.

"Yeah... Belle's told me what happened. She had no right to ask you to run her errands in the first place, and she was bang out of order talking to you like that. I'm sorry."

"You've got nothing to apologise for. It's fine, anyway. They've promised delivery on Saturday so– "

"All right, but I'll go over and collect it..." He pauses for a moment and frowns. "Are you really okay?"

"Honestly, I'm fine. There's something I want to ask you, though. I wondered if I could have the night off. I'd like to meet Caz and Janine for a drink at the pub, if you can manage without me?"

"Sure, that's a great idea, and it's a teacher training day tomorrow, so I was planning on taking Toby up to the stables in the morning. Why don't you take the morning off – have a lay-in or something?"

"Thanks, that sounds brilliant."

For the first time, Matt smiles. It's gentle and reassuring and I finally let go of the remnants of tension I've been holding onto.

"Good, I'm glad that's settled." His eyes capture mine.

"I'd better go and pickup Toby." I croak out, but my legs don't move.

Matt's feet seem stuck to the floor too, as he continues to regard me. After a moment, he nods and turns away, freeing me from his mesmerising eyes. I take a deep, steadying breath and grab my car keys to collect Toby from school.

Chapter 23 – Rosie

My-Name-Is-Toby–NOT–Tobias…

Excitement at the thought of a night out with my girls has replaced my earlier stress with Belle. And no alarm clock in the morning - perfect.

Before all of that, though, Toby and I are busy in the kitchen making homemade pizzas for tea. I've got a selection of toppings, and Toby's standing on a step stool so he can choose which ones he wants before carefully placing them on his pizza base.

Matt's sitting at the kitchen table, his laptop open and a coffee at his side. Belle's still using his office, but he seems content to be with us. He listens while I ask Toby about his school day, and we chat about the important issue of whether you can have *too many* toppings on a pizza.

"Dad, are you having pizza too?" Toby looks up from his task and pops a slice of tomato into his mouth.

"Umm, I'd love a pizza if there's enough?" Matt lifts his eyes at me in question.

"Sure is – do you want to add your own toppings, or should Toby do it?"

"Me! Me! Me!" Toby squawks like an over excited parrot.

"Guess Toby better do it." Matt winks at me just as Belle comes into the kitchen.

"What a lot of noise, Tobias." Though rather than looking at him, she directs her disapproval at me.

"My-Name-Is-Toby–NOT–Tobias." Toby emphasises each word while looking sternly at Belle.

My heart sinks. I hope this isn't going to turn into an awkward confrontation, but then Matt rises from his chair and walks towards the fridge.

"Belle, have a glass of wine and relax. We're having pizzas - do you want one?"

"Uh, no, thanks. I thought we might try that new French Bistro. The reviews are excellent."

"Can't, I'm afraid. Rosie's got the night off, so I'm on Toby duty."

I nervously wait for her reaction, but she simply nods and takes the white wine he offers her. Abruptly, Matt's mobile rings, the sound cutting through the awkward atmosphere. He answers the call while striding purposefully out of the kitchen.

While Toby's oblivious to the changed atmosphere, I can tell that Belle's simmering with resentment towards me for ruining her plans. She sips her wine slowly, and I tentatively wait for what she'll say next, because I'm sure she's not going to let me off the hook easily.

"When did you arrange your night off?" Her eyes glint with annoyance.

"This afternoon. I asked Matt earlier, and he said it was okay."

"Is it not customary and polite to give at least a few days' prior notice to your employer when requesting time off?"

"I... I'm sorry. It was a spur-of-the-moment thing. I mean, I'd have completely understood if Matt had said no."

Belle continues to sip her wine. I know she wants me to back down and cancel my night out. She intimidates the hell out of me and maybe I should cancel, if only to prevent this horrible atmosphere. Just then, Matt breezes back into the kitchen, and I take a shaky breath, making my mind up.

"Matt, I didn't realise you had plans to go out this evening. I can easily go out another time."

His eyes travel between me and Belle, taking in the tension between us. "Don't be daft. It's all arranged. That was Harry on the phone. He's going to drop you girls off at the pub and then come here for the evening."

He grins, and relief wraps around me because he's being so sweet and caring, though I fear I've made things much worse between Belle and me. She's unlikely to forgive me for disrupting her evening, and I'm scared to think of what the consequences of that might be.

Chapter 24 – Rosie

Call me a bitch…

"Here's to us." We raise and clink glasses.

"And for nearly surviving another week - at least there's no school tomorrow, so the weekend can start early." Janine sighs. "Maybe Olly will even let me lie in tomorrow and not get me up at 'silly o'clock' time."

It's 8 p.m., and the pub is pleasantly busy with regulars and a few tourists enjoying a drink in the beer garden, making the most of the last of the evening sunshine. We're sitting at a table inside where it's quieter and we can chat, away from the noise of families with boisterous children running around outside.

Caz is dressed in a black silk taffeta dress with a full ruffled skirt and draped across her shoulders is an orange crushed velvet wrap. Heavy black kohl pencil emphasises her almond-shaped eyes and her hair is up, secured with a diamanté clip; long curling tendrils framing her face. I love her quirky style, which reminds me a bit of Helena Bonham Carter.

Janine and I have opted for a more conventional look. Janine's wearing a denim pinafore jumpsuit with a Breton style navy blue stripe top. It's fun and trendy, just like her, and it suits her. I've chosen a short ditsy floral print dress teamed with a denim jacket for later in case it turns chilly. Ever practical me!

"Sooo…" Caz draws out the letters. "How did your date go with the gorgeous Liam?" She looks across at Janine, and I can already tell from her body language that the date went well.

"It was supposed to be a coffee at the community café after class, but we ended up having lunch and then we went for a walk before I needed to get back for Olly. It was lovely. He's so nice and easy to talk to."

"Pretty easy on the eye, too." Caz winks at her.

Pink flushes Janine's cheeks, "Yes, well, that too."

"And will there be a second date?"

"He wants to take me out Saturday night for dinner. Only thing is I need a babysitter, and I can't ask my neighbour again as she's looking after Olly tonight." Janine looks at me with pleading eyes.

"Why don't I pick Olly up about 4 o'clock, and he can come to ours for tea and a sleepover? That'll give you loads of time to get ready, and you'll have a child-free evening." I smile back at her.

"Well, that's all settled then." Caz beams. "I love a bit of romance. Talking of which, how's Matt?"

"He's fine," I reply, trying to keep my voice neutral.

"Harry and I bumped into Belle and him at the pub last night. I'm not sure a burger and chips are really Belle's style, though. How are you getting on with her?"

I'm tempted to confide that I don't think she likes me and doesn't approve of me being Toby's nanny. But I'd feel awful if my gossiping got back to Matt, so I decide discretion is needed.

"Oh, okay. I mean, I don't see a lot of her, really."

"So, is she here for good?" Janine asks me.

The idea of Matt and Belle being together permanently is – well, too unsettling to think about. "I really don't know. She's sleeping in the guest room at the moment, but that might be because Matt doesn't want Toby to know they're together yet."

Caz looks at me shrewdly through her dark, smoky eyes. "Well, I don't like her. There I've said it. Call me a bitch, but goodness knows what Matt sees in her."

I can't help laughing. "Caz!"

"Whhaatt? I'd hazard a guess that you don't like her much either. You're just far too polite to say so."

"So why don't you like her?" Janine looks between us, curiosity written all over her face.

"I just don't think she's right for him. She's such a snob with her 'I'm better than you' attitude. Harry doesn't get it either. He thinks she must be great in bed."

The image of Belle whispering intimately into Matt's ear earlier and trailing her fingers over his neck possessively flashes through my mind. Jealousy, like a solid heavy weight, squeezes my stomach.

"I really don't want to think about that. Let's change the subject. So, any singing gigs lined up?" I ask Caz, hoping she'll take the hint.

"Matt's asked me to perform a few numbers at the Summer Ball."

"The what?" we both chime at once, looking at Caz in surprise.

"It's a charity event that's held every year in the summer at the centre. Everyone dresses up and there's a fancy meal, a charity auction and dancing into the early hours. It's very popular, and there are always more people wanting to go than tickets."

"Wow, that sounds amazing," Janine exclaims before I can reply.

"Yes, that sounds amazing," I repeat, imagining being twirled around the dance floor by Matt, his intense dark eyes focused on me alone.

I realise with a jolt that Caz's eyes are studying me, and I shift uncomfortably in my seat at the idea she's somehow reading my inappropriate thoughts. But she whispers, "Tom, behind the bar, has been eyeing you all evening. I think he fancies you."

Abandoning my little daydream, I take a subtle eye sweep towards the bar. Tom's indeed looking at me, and his lips turn up into a wide grin when he notices I'm returning his stare.

"Why don't you go over?" Janine nudges me. "I'm sure he's interested in you."

I groan inwardly and wonder if I'm being set up. I wouldn't put it past them both to have planned this, but then I decide what the hell. Tom's good looking (even if he clearly knows it) and I haven't been on a date in a very long time. It might do me good, and it'll certainly get Matt off my mind.

"I'll get another bottle of wine." I walk over to the bar, feeling their eyes on me.

"Hi Tom, another bottle of house red, please."

He's around my age with a surfer's look of mushed up dark-blond hair, blue eyes and perfect white teeth. Boyishly handsome and flirty, he obviously doesn't need to work hard for his dates. We stand chatting and I become the focus of his well-used chat-up lines, but I can't help laughing at some of his cheesy jokes. Rather surprising myself, we swap numbers and I agree to a dinner date with him the following week.

By the time I return to my seat, Caz and Janine are agog with curiosity, and I brace myself for the inevitable teasing that's bound to follow once they know I've agreed to a date. But then doubt niggles at me as I wonder if I've done the right thing, but I'll look ridiculous if I back out now. Anyway, a date with Tom will distract me from thinking about Matt all the time, and that's got to be a good thing.

The evening sun slowly disappears into the shadowy twilight. We drink more delicious wine, laughing and gossiping together until last orders are called and lovely, dependable Harry arrives to taxi us all home.

Chapter 25 – Matt

Don't be ridiculous, she's Toby's nanny.

I see Harry every day at work, but it's been quite a while since we've hung out together properly. He embraces me in his usual strong bear hug and we go into the sitting room, where the TV's located, and we can watch the football match being shown tonight.

Belle excuses herself from our sports fest, expressing the desire for a hot bath and early night, and disappears upstairs with the rest of the opened bottle of wine from earlier.

Harry lies stretched out on one of the big leather sofas, along the length of one wall, while I commandeer the other sofa on the adjoining wall. After our drinks are sorted – beer for me and a soft drink for Harry, as he's driving later to collect the girls - we settle down to our evening's entertainment.

Frustratingly, the match is rubbish – neither side setting the game on fire despite Harry and I repeatedly yelling our 'expert' advice at the TV screen. The referee blows his whistle for half-time, and I get up to find more snacks and Harry follows me into the kitchen.

"So, is Belle shacked up here for good?" Harry looks at me questioningly, as I tear open a large family size bag of crisps and shake them into a bowl.

"No, in fact, quite the opposite. It was a stupid mistake to get together in the first place and now – well, let's just say I've come to my senses. She's just staying here for a few more days as a favour until her builder finishes at her flat."

"Oh, I see. How's she taken it?"

I shrug. "Not great. I shouldn't have let it drag on for so long, but she'll be okay once she realises she's better off with one of her wealthy admirers."

"I'm sorry, mate."

"It's fine. Belle and I weren't ever going anywhere long term."

Harry smiles at me sympathetically. "The right woman's out there for you. What about Rosie? She's gorgeous and much more your type."

"Don't be ridiculous, she's Toby's nanny." I squeeze my eyes shut and then open them again. "Anyway, I'm really crap at relationships. Toby and I are best off on our own."

"So, what if she's Toby's nanny? I mean, who cares if she works for you. Lots of people get together like that. You're overthinking it, mate. She's exactly what you need."

I brush off Harry with my usual scowl. I know Harry wants to see me happy, like he is with Caz, but how can I let myself get involved with anyone when I'm so weighed down with guilt and regret about the past?

Harry smiles ruefully at me as we wander back to our respective sofas and carry on sharing our pundit advice to the hapless football players for the rest of the match.

Chapter 26 – Rosie

You haven't seen a pretty green ring lying around, have you?

There's nothing more wonderfully self-indulgent than a long lie-in when the rest of the household is awake and busy. I stretch out in bed, luxuriating in my morning of freedom, and wonder if I should go back to sleep or treat myself to breakfast in bed, followed by a bubble bath and manicure. As I contemplate my morning's schedule, I doze off again until I'm gently lulled awake by Toby's distinctive laughter floating up from the drive, below my bedroom window.

A soft eiderdown of contentment wraps itself around me as I listen, and I wonder what's made Toby so amused. I slip out of bed and move the bedroom curtain a smidgen, so I can secretly spy on whatever is happening outside. Toby's walking between Belle and Matt, and every so often they swing him high off his feet to delighted whoops of joy as he flies through the air. Of course, they're holding on tight to his skinny arms, so he's in no danger of falling, but the jeopardy of it thrills Toby all the same.

I watch as they make their way up the driveway to the stables. Matt's laughing at something, his face lit up with amusement, and abruptly Toby lets go of their hands and bounds ahead skipping and running, his zest for life bursting out of him. Belle links her arm with Matt's, and they walk along together looking like a perfect, happy family. I watch transfixed until they disappear from view and then I drag myself back to bed, curling up into a tight ball under the duvet cover, as a cruel ache of jealousy steals my mood.

***

After my little blip this morning, I'm back on track with my 'get over Matt' strategy, and I've decided the only way to do that is to embrace my upcoming date with Tom. I've booked a hair appointment, and I'm going to treat myself to a new outfit. With any luck, my date will help me finally get over my stupid infatuation with Matt.

Toby's back in my charge after his morning at the riding centre, and we're both at the kitchen table eating a sandwich lunch while he tells me all about his exciting time.

"Dad, let me take the reins for a minute, and he's going to teach me how to use them. He even said I can have proper riding lessons soon."

His face is so animated and full of enthusiasm, I can't help joining in with his excitement. "That's awesome, Toby. I bet you were brilliant."

"Dad says I've still got lots to learn about feeding and grooming. Dad's going to let me help him during the school holidays. I've got to get up early, though."

"I'm sure we can set an alarm, so you get up in time. How about we do some sketches after lunch - you could draw a picture of the horse you were riding and give it to your dad as a surprise?"

Just then, I hear raised voices coming from Matt's office. The door's ajar and it's clear that Belle and Matt are arguing about something.

"Don't be ridiculous," Matt snaps.

"All I'm saying is that I left my ring on my bedside table this morning, and it's not there now."

"Well, I'm sure there's a perfectly reasonable explanation."

"Oh yes, like it's grown legs and walked off on its own."

"Like I say, you're being ridiculous. Maybe you accidentally knocked it off the table. Have you checked under your bed?" I can hear exasperation in Matt's voice.

"Yes, of course, and I've searched the rest of the bedroom, too. I can only think that someone's taken it."

The office door bangs shut. I can no longer hear any talking, but my stomach clenches with fear at the inference Belle's making. If her ring's missing and I was the only person in the house this morning, does she think I took it? I wait nervously, dreading what will happen next, and I don't have long to wait because Belle walks into the kitchen with Matt following close behind.

Belle's eyes narrow on me. "I've lost a very expensive emerald and diamond ring, and I wondered if you've seen it?"

Matt glares at her and then his dark eyes lock onto mine, full of apology.

"No, I'm sorry I haven't seen your ring, but I can search around if you like?" I do my best to keep my voice calm, but my heart is jackhammering against my ribcage.

"It's okay, Rosie. I'll check Belle's room in a minute. It's probably fallen down behind her bedside table." Matt smiles at me, but I don't return it. "Toby, you haven't seen a pretty green ring lying around, have you?"

"No, dad, but I can look in my bedroom if you like."

"No, there's no need, buddy." Matt ruffles Toby's hair, and I think he's about to say something else when Belle speaks again.

"Perhaps you could look in *your* room, nanny?"

She stares at me and there's blatant accusation in her eyes, but before I can respond, Matt growls, "There's absolutely no need for that, Rosie. I'm sure we'll find it."

I nod at him, trying to ignore Belle's obvious insinuation, but she might as well have come right out with it. She thinks I'm a thief. And even if I can convince her I'm not in fact guilty of pilfering her precious ring, she's made no secret of her dislike of me so, if she's living here permanently, she'll only increase hostilities.

I suddenly think the unthinkable... it's an insidious, unwanted thought, but now I can't push it away. *I don't have a future here.* The truth cuts through me like sharp razor blades and, all at once, it feels like I don't have enough oxygen in my lungs to breathe.

Matt's face tightens with worry, and he gently touches my shoulder with his hand. "Are you okay, Rosie? You look a bit–"

"I'm fine." I cut him off. "I'll keep an eye out for your ring, Belle." Shaking off Matt's hand, I get up and walk over to the sink to get a glass of water.

"For fuck's sake, Belle," Matt barks out, but when I look up, she's already left the room, the door slamming violently behind her.

"Dad, you've just said a naughty word." Toby's eyes are round with surprise. "Daniel Hardcastle wasn't allowed playtime last week, because he said that word to the dinner lady. She'd told him to eat his broccoli, but he said he didn't like broccoli and when she offered him cauliflower instead, he told her to fu–."

"–Yes, okay, Toby," Matt interrupts. "You're quite right, it's a very naughty word, and I shouldn't have said it." He sighs heavily and comes to stand next to me by the sink, but I can't bring myself to look at him. "Rosie, are you sure you're okay?"

"Honestly, I'm fine," I mumble towards his shirt collar. I want to sound reassuring, because I can't deal with the reality of my thoughts right now. I take a shaky breath, willing myself not to cry.

"Belle's behaviour was totally unacceptable." His voice is gentle, but I refuse to meet his eyes.

"It's fine," I croak out again, but nothing could be further from the truth.

I've had a sense of foreboding for a few days and now I know why. If Belle's here to stay, then I realise I need to leave… my job, my home and, worst of all, Matt and Toby.

Chapter 27 – Matt

What's the difference between broccoli and cauliflower?

I hate that word *fine*. It's such an insipid, meaningless word, and any fool could see that Rosie was anything but *fine*. I watch as she swigs back a glass of water and then, outwardly at least, she seems to regain her composure. Ignoring me, she walks back over to Toby and, taking him by his hand, they both go outside to sit at the patio table.

Toby's a master joke teller and, after his little revelation about Daniel Hardcastle, he's in his absolute element, showing off his full repertoire of vegetable themed jokes to Rosie. Being six years old, he's also his own most appreciative audience because he finds all his jokes hilarious. And I mean belly-laughing, side-splitting, cracking-up-funny hilarious, which is precisely how he's acting now.

"What's the difference between broccoli and cauliflower? Cauliflower is just broccoli that's seen a ghost!

What type of flower shouldn't be put in a vase? A cauliflower!

If you've got four cauliflowers in one hand and six cabbages in the other hand, what do you have? Big hands!"

Rosie's grinning broadly and, when she finally lifts her eyes to meet mine, I mouth back 'thank you' because she's not only entertaining my son, but she's also resetting the mood from the toxic atmosphere Belle had created earlier.

The sound of their laughter echoes around the kitchen and, not for the first time, I realise how fortunate Toby and I are to have Rosie in our lives. On the other hand, Belle's behaviour towards Rosie has been appalling and, as I go in search of her stupid ring, I decide enough is enough.

***

I found the ring in Belle's ensuite. It was in a small bin containing discarded makeup wipes. She must have been taking off her makeup, and the ring had somehow slipped off her finger and got tangled up in a tissue by mistake. I can tell that the ring's expensive and I'm relieved I've found it, but I'm also annoyed at Belle's behaviour. She'd virtually accused Rosie of stealing it, and I decide in that moment that I've been patient long enough, and Belle needs to leave immediately, whether or not her flat is ready. She'll have to check in to a hotel, if necessary, but she can't stay here any longer.

Belle walks into the bedroom just as I'm exiting her ensuite. I walk over and hand her the ring. "You've found it – oh, thank goodness. Gosh, where was it?" She glances at the emerald ring and then back up at me, smiling.

"It was in the bin in your ensuite. Somehow it got wrapped up in a makeup wipe." I glare at her.

"Oh, thank you. I didn't think I'd ever see it again. You know it's worth a lot of money."

"I don't care how much it's worth. What's important is that you more or less accused Rosie of stealing it. You can't go around accusing people like that."

"I didn't." Her voice is petulant.

"You implied it, and Rosie hasn't done anything to deserve your suspicion or the vitriol you continually dish out to her."

"I don't know what you mean."

"Don't you? Anyway, you owe her an apology," I snap, suddenly tired of our pointless backwards and forwards.

Belle looks at me carefully through her dark lashes, clearly calculating whether to argue the point but then thinks better of it. "Yes, of course. I'll go to see her right away." She wraps her arms round my neck and goes to kiss me, but I take a step back, forcing her to drop her arms once more to her side.

"I know I agreed you could stay until the builder finishes at your flat, but I want you to leave." I look at her, and I'm shocked to see tears spilling down her face. I've never seen her cry – she's always so feisty and confident.

"I'm so sorry." Her tears are flowing harder. "I really thought – Oh God – I'm sorry. I'll make it up to you, I promise. Please, Matt…" She trails off, swallowing down a sob.

I clench my jaw in frustration, because I've never been able to handle a woman crying. It feels altogether wrong, and my earlier resolve seeps away as she lets out another painful sob.

"Belle, you're only staying here as a friend, nothing more. I won't change my mind about us being together. Do you understand that?"

"Yes, of course." Her voice is small and contrite. "I promise I'll make this up to you if you'll let me."

I wonder why she's so keen to remain here. Surely, she still doesn't harbour any hope I'll change my mind about us even though I'd made it clear at the pub that our relationship, such as it was, is over. But then I realise how much effort she's been making; possessive, almost territorial, displays of affection that leave me feeling awkward whenever Rosie's witnessed them for some reason. But I push that unsettling thought away.

"You need to apologise to Rosie. That's a start, I suppose." I walk out of the bedroom, furious with myself that I've once again allowed Belle to have her own way.

Chapter 28 – Rosie

A pendulum of indecision…

Belle's apology feels hollow and insincere, and I'm sure Matt put her up to it.

It also feels like the final straw. First, her insistence that Toby should have a qualified nanny and now the missing ring fiasco. The last thing I want is to leave, but what choice do I have? The confident, possessive way Belle acts around Matt only confirms she's become a permanent fixture here and, while Matt may have forced her into apologising this time (and this battle may be over), in my gut I know the war is only just beginning.

Reluctantly, I begin carefully scanning the nanny job vacancies and updating my C.V., such as it is. I decide London's my best option. There are many more jobs there, and a recent advertisement catches my eye. It's working for a family with two pre-school children, and the mum's pregnant with baby number three due imminently. They want a nanny urgently, so maybe they'll be more open to hiring someone like me, without very much experience.

I complete the online application, but then I hesitate. A pendulum of indecision swings back and forth in my head as I contemplate leaving Matt and Toby. *I can't do it.* Even though I've only been living here a short time, it feels like home and a place where I belong. It had been such a long time since I'd felt like that. I'd had a family once, and I'd been loved, but then everything had been ripped apart when… but I push the dark intrusive thoughts away.

My finger hovers over the send button but finally, taking a shaky breath, I press it. The email disappears into the ether, and aching sadness and regret squeeze my heart so tightly it feels like it's going to break. I close my eyes in misery as a big, fat tear slides down my face and lands on my laptop. My life's in flux again, and I feel more alone that I've ever felt before.

Chapter 29 – Matt

I-want-you-here–Rosie…

What the hell.

Some recruitment agency has just rung me asking for a reference for Rosie and now I'm furious, red-hot anger raging through me, and I want to punch the nearest wall.

"Rosie!" I bellow from my office, even though I know she and Toby are only across the hallway in the kitchen.

Rosie walks into my office, and I can tell by her body language she's worked out I know she's applied for another job. Her head's down, and her eyes are fixed on the floor in embarrassment. She's waiting for me to say something, but my temper is so close to the surface I can't trust myself to speak coherently. I take a couple of steadying breaths, trying to calm down while I continue staring at her. She's nervous, like a captured bird in a cage desperately wanting to take flight, and I feel my anger evaporating, replaced with hurt and confusion.

"Rosie, what's going on? I've had a recruitment agency on the 'phone asking for a reference for you – some job looking after two children and a baby in London."

"I've applied for another job." She slowly raises her head, her eyes meeting mine.

"Why would you do that?"

"I can't stay here." Her voice is so low I can hardly hear her.

"Why on earth not?"

Suddenly, her voice breaks. "I know Belle's your girlfriend, but she's made it very clear what she thinks of me, and it's making my life impossible."

"I'm so sorry about the misunderstanding over that stupid ring. Belle was way out of order".

"It's not just that." Rosie hesitates, and I see a wave of indecision sweep across her face about whether she should say more.

"Tell me." I say firmly.

She exhales a shaky breath, and when she speaks again, her voice is flat and resigned. "I think you need someone with professional childcare qualifications to look after Toby."

"That sounds like Belle talking, not you." I keep my voice calm, but my anger is back, because I realise this is all about Belle trying to control and manipulate.

Rosie's gaze drops to the floor again. "I don't think she'll ever be happy with me being here." She gulps down a sob.

"Come here." I take her arm, gently guiding her over to me, and tip her chin up with my index finger so I can see into her beautiful eyes, the colour of the summer sky. I take a deep breath, trying to keep my anger in check and my voice even.

"First, it's none of Belle's damn business who I hire. Second, if I wasn't happy with our domestic arrangements, I'd tell you myself. Third, Toby worships you, and he's happier than I've ever seen him – and his happiness is always my main priority. And, finally, you're doing an amazing job and I-want-you-here–Rosie." I emphasise the last five words slowly.

Rosie's eyes shimmer with tears, and I watch her searching my face for the truth in my words.

"I love it here."

I don't let go of her eyes. "Then stay, please."

She nods slowly, and I fight the urge to take her into my arms to comfort her. "Anyway, I've already told the agency to bugger off." I wink at her. "So, are we good now?"

She suddenly hiccups and gives me a watery smile. "We're good."

"And if anything's ever bothering you, please tell me first. I need you to be honest with me, okay?"

Rosie bites down on her bottom lip and arches an eyebrow. "Okay… umm… well, there is just one small thing. Please stop making me coffee. I really hate the stuff."

"What?" I can't believe what I'm hearing. "But I've made you countless cups of coffee since you've been here."

"I know, but most of it usually ends up being thrown down the sink." Her mouth turns into a playful grin.

I squeeze the back of my neck, trying to get my head around her confession. "Okay, no more coffee…anything else?"

"No, thanks, we're good, Matt. I'd…umm…I'd better get back to Toby."

"Yeah, okay."

I watch as Rosie walks towards the door and relief floods through me she's staying. But there's something else too – an intense attraction - and my body's reacting, the only way it knows how. I wonder what it would be like to feel her mouth against mine, to steal her breath…but then I come to my senses. She's my employee and completely off limits. Not only that, but I have a cynical heart that distrusts love and commitment. I close my eyes and grit down hard on my jaw as conflicting emotions battle inside me.

Chapter 30 – Rosie

I know how fragile and transient happiness is…

After my heart to heart with Matt, I feel much happier and that I might be better off growing a backbone to stand up to all of Belle's nonsense. Fight rather than flight…well, that's the plan, anyway.

After all the drama of the last couple of days, I suddenly remember that I'd offered to have Olly for a sleepover tonight so Janine and Liam can go on their dinner date. Thankfully Matt's chilled about it and after Toby and I have collected Olly, we stop off on the way home to watch the horses grazing peacefully in the paddock by the stables, their coats gleaming with good health, their long tails swishing occasionally as if warning away any curious visiting insects. The late afternoon sun warms my skin, as I relax against the fence listening to the boys' excited chatter. Matt's doing a BBQ later and my only job is to keep the boys entertained and hopefully stop them from getting up to too much mischief.

After a while, we leave the horses to their tranquil reverie and drive the short distance home. I see Matt's prepping the BBQ on the patio, but there's no sign of Belle, which I can't help feeling thankful for.

"Toby, take Olly up to your room and show him where he's sleeping. Then both of you wash your hands and I'll call you when tea's ready." The boys nod at me like angelic choir boys and disappear upstairs while I go into the garden to see if I can help Matt.

"Belle's out to dinner with a prospective client. Though I suspect that's an excuse because she doesn't fancy entertaining two six-year-olds." Matt turns to face me, his mouth forming into a gorgeous smile as his deep brown eyes meet mine.

I smile back at him, and my stomach constricts as his dark eyes continue to observe me. He's wearing grey cotton shorts and a faded black T-shirt which shows off his abs perfectly. His dark ruffled hair and five-o'clock shadow are way too sexy and distracting, and I take a gulp of air, trying to clear my head.

Reluctantly, I turn away and busy myself setting out plates and condiments. Then I grab some rolls and salad from the kitchen to go with the sausages, burgers and chicken Matt's grilling. It's the perfect evening for a BBQ and I put my phone on speaker and select my favourite tracks to play in the background.

As if sensing the food's almost ready, the boys magically appear, and I take their small hands in mine and begin twirling them around to the hypnotic Abba music. I know all the classic hits by heart, and I sing along to the lyrics as the boys giggle and sway their hips to the familiar catchy rhythm.

Then the song changes to a slower tempo, and I remember another time when I'd danced like this. A whispered memory from the past floats into my mind of an older boy who'd spun me around and around. Beautiful, funny, happy memories…

The lyrics are poignant; a lost war, but no regrets. Unlike the song, I have so many regrets and tears threaten, as I think of the older boy who'd fought in a different conflict and made the ultimate sacrifice. Then the track changes again to a more upbeat one and chases the memory away.

I'm a dancing diva and the boys and I flail and whirl our arms in time to the music. A burst of happiness swells my heart, as I notice Matt's wide grin as he watches us, and I want to lock this moment away in my memory forever, because I know how fragile and transient happiness is.

And when the music stops, like the dusky evening light, my happiness fades away because the one thing I want more than anything is the one thing I cannot have.

Chapter 31 – Rosie

You both sound like a pair of fishwives…

The BBQ's a great success and by 8 p.m. all the food's been demolished, sticky fingers and faces washed, and two sleepy boys tucked up in bed. Not bad, even if I say so myself. After the boys are asleep, I escape to my room, so when Belle gets back, she and Matt can spend the rest of their evening alone.

After breakfast, I take Olly home and quickly grab an update from Janine on her romantic night-out with Liam. She's loved-up and happy, and I'm pleased her blossoming love-life's going so well. At least she has one, I grumble to myself.

"Where's Toby?" I scan the kitchen as I walk in, but there's no sign of him.

"Belle's taken him up to the stables to feed the horses." Matt hands me a mug of tea and then concentrates on making his own drink from the complicated coffee machine.

"Are you sure that's a good idea?" I blurt out. Belle's not exactly known for her child friendly qualities, though I refrain from saying that.

"She offered to take him, and he wanted to go so… Anyway, they won't be long."

My stomach suddenly grips with fear. "Are they going riding?" I stare coldly at him and steel myself for his answer.

"No, of course not." He returns my stare, which says I'm being ridiculous. "I know I took him out the other day, but she wouldn't put him on a horse without me."

"Oh, well, I guess that's okay then." Though I'm still not convinced - I mean, it's Belle we're talking about.

"Relax, Rosie. Have an hour of peace in the garden." I nod as he gives me a reassuring smile before disappearing into his office with his coffee.

I huff out a sigh and grab my book and sunglasses and wander out into the garden. I guess I'm overreacting, but the idea of Toby spending any time alone with Belle makes me uneasy. Still, I guess if Matt's not worried, I should take his advice and relax.

I lie down on one of the garden recliners and close my eyes. It's a perfect blue, cloudless sky, and the heat from the sun warms me. My eyes grow heavy and I lazily drift off to sleep, letting my book fall.

***

"DAAAD… ROSIE… DAAAD…"I'm aware someone shouting my name. Disorientated, I slowly open my eyes, trying to adjust to the bright sunlight. The noise is coming from the drive and then Toby bursts into the garden and runs towards me. At the same time, Matt emerges from the kitchen looking as confused as I am.

Toby's hysterical, shouting my name over and over again as he launches himself straight onto my lap and puts his thin arms around my neck, clinging on like a Koala Bear. I hug him to me and stroke his back, trying to comfort him.

"It's okay, honey." I whisper into his neck. "I'm here, and dad's here. It's okay."

Matt stands over me and ruffles Toby's hair, just as Belle arrives with a grim expression on her face.

"Tobias, stop being such a baby," she scolds him firmly.

Toby's cries have calmed to a whimper, but he's still holding onto me tightly, burying his face into my neck.

"What happened?" Matt demands.

Belle walks over to Matt, ignoring Toby and me, and places her hand on his arm. "Tobias was messing about, and he fell. It really wasn't anything major – honestly, he's just being a baby. I told him to get right back on again, but he started crying and demanded to come home."

"What do you mean, he fell?" Matt's eyes are thunderous as he glares at her.

"I thought a short ride around the paddock would be fun." Belle's face is belligerent.

"What? I specifically told you not to take him riding." Matt's voice is icily calm, and I think he's about to say more, but then he turns to Toby.

"Are you hurt, buddy? Does anywhere hurt?"

Toby shakes his head, but he's still whimpering against me. I suddenly decide I've had enough of all this pandemonium, so I carefully lift him up and his small legs wrap around my waist as I take him upstairs to his room.

"Did you hurt yourself?" I ask gently, as I lay him on his bed and sit down beside him. Matt's followed me upstairs, and he sits down too, as Toby sniffs and shakes his head.

"I was a bit scared, and then Belle said I needed to get back on and I didn't want to. I just wanted to come home."

"That's okay. I'm so sorry you had a fall. Are you sure nowhere hurts?"

He shakes his head again, as we both scan him for any obvious signs of injury.

My heart's thumping with adrenaline and anger, but I don't know if it's anger at Belle for failing to keep Toby safe or Matt for letting him go with Belle in the first place. As if he senses it, Matt reaches for my hand and squeezes it.

"I'll make Toby a drink," I murmur, as I rise from the bed, pulling my hand away.

I walk downstairs, white hot rage burning into each step I take, and I find Belle standing in the kitchen nonchalantly drinking coffee. "I can't believe you were so reckless and stupid. How could you let this happen?" My voice is incandescent with fury.

"I won't be told off by you," Belle retorts, her flashing green eyes drilling into me.

"Toby could have been seriously hurt, or worse. He's 6 years old. What the hell were you thinking, not supervising him properly?" I'm shouting now, livid anger boiling up uncontrollably inside me.

"How dare you speak to me like that!" Belle yells back.

"Enough! You both sound like a pair of fishwives," Matt booms from the doorway.

I'm about to reply, but Matt interrupts me. "My office now," he barks, brooking no argument.

Chapter 32 – Matt

I'm sorry…

"What on earth were you thinking?" I try to keep my voice level, but it's taking every bit of control I have. My knuckles turn white as I grip the edge of the kitchen table hard, attempting to stop myself from losing my temper.

"I know, I know. I'm sorry. I just wanted to do something nice, and I thought if Tobias had a good time riding, you'd…" Belle stops mid-sentence, her unsaid words floating in the air between us.

"I'd what?" I ask, confused.

"It doesn't matter."

"Yes, I think it does very much matter. What were you about to say?"

Belle swallows, and her eyes fix onto mine. "I thought that I'd be able to prove to you how good we'd be together as a family."

I stare at her for a long moment, trying to make sense of her admission, and she interrupts my jumbled thoughts.

"I mean, I'd hoped you'd give me…us another chance. We could be great together, Matt."

"Belle, I– "

"I'm sorry. I'm so very sorry that I took Tobias riding, without telling you. Truly I am."

I rake my hand through my hair, ice-cold resolve hardening inside me, while she continues to plead with me.

Chapter 33 – Rosie

I absolutely won't apologise.

I march into Matt's office and sit defiantly on his desk, swinging my legs. Childish behaviour, but I'm beyond caring. I can hear Belle and him talking, and a few minutes later, Matt walks in and shuts the door.

He stops in front of me, his body tantalisingly close to mine, his face full of concern. The urge to touch him, to breathe him in, is overwhelming. But I'm angry too, and the anger wins. Uneven breaths stumble out of me, and I can't hold back my temper any longer.

"I'm not sorry for shouting at her. She deserves everything I said to her, and I absolutely won't apologise."

"I'm not going to ask you to apologise. I actually agree with everything you said. Belle should have been far more careful."

A sob escapes my throat as the seriousness of the situation hits me once again. "He might have been seriously injured, or worse." I shut my eyes, and a single tear falls down my cheek, which Matt gently wipes away with the pad of his thumb.

"I know, but thankfully, he's okay," Matt says softly.

"But he might not have been," I retort stubbornly. "What if…."

Matt pulls me towards him, wrapping me in his arms. "No more what ifs."

I breathe out shakily and slowly open my eyes. He's resting his forehead gently against the top of my head, and I feel his heart beating steadily in his chest. His hand moves slowly up and down my tense back, and it calms my strung-out nerves.

After a moment, he pulls away and his eyes find mine. "I've told Belle to go. She's just packing." I gulp down my surprise and scramble around in my head for a suitable reply. Maybe I should say I'm sorry she's leaving, but I'd be a liar because I'm not sorry at all.

I take a slow, steadying breath. "I … I'd better get back to Toby."

Matt only nods, so I make my way towards the door. Then he calls out. "Rosie …" I turn round to look at him, and our eyes lock.

"It doesn't matter."

I wonder what he was about to say and why he'd changed his mind, but his face is inscrutable.

Chapter 34- Matt

I'm sure you'll find the perfect boyfriend soon…

I feel nothing but relief at Belle's departure. I couldn't forgive that she'd put Toby in danger and, though she'd pleaded with me, this time I wouldn't change my mind.

For my part, I'd made a huge error of judgement over my casual hook-ups with Belle. We'd used each other, but then Belle had changed her mind and, to my shame, I'd hurt her when I wouldn't commit to a more serious relationship, and she didn't deserve that. I also realise she'd contrived to stay here in the hope I'd reconsider. I'd handled the whole situation badly, and the resulting mess was entirely on me.

Last night, I'd almost told Rosie that Belle and I hadn't been together for months, and she was only staying here as a favour. But then I'd thought better of it, because why would she even care?

Thankfully, Toby seems none the worse for his experience. I watch him and Rosie from the kitchen, as they sit sketching at the patio table in the garden. Toby's pushed his chair as close to Rosie's as he can, and he's listening completely riveted to something she's saying. Then he bursts out laughing with one of his familiar loud, full on belly laughs, and that makes Rosie giggle too. She looks up, smiling, and winks at me.

I return her smile, and warmth fills the cold void where my heart used to be. Rosie's the promise of spring after the long winter; of sunshine after heavy rain. I'm not worthy of her smile, though. I'm an arse and, after the way I've treated Belle, not someone to trust with your heart.

***

"You look lovely – off anywhere nice?"

I turn towards Rosie as she comes into the sitting room. She's dressed in a light blue summer dress that brings out the beautiful colour of her sapphire eyes and her glossy golden hair hangs loosely over her shoulders. Her brown shapely legs are encased in espadrilles wedges which increase her height by several inches, but I still tower above her when I get up from the sofa. I notice she's wearing her usual pink lip gloss and I idly wonder what it would taste of if I put my mouth over hers, which is ridiculous as her date is with Tom from the pub, so she'll obviously be kissing him later rather than me.

"We're going to that new French Bistro that Belle was talking about. I shouldn't be late, though."

I wonder if she knows that her date has a reputation for 'love'em and leave'em' one-night stands. Ironically, before Belle came on the scene, one-night stands were my modus operandi too, so I can hardly judge him. All the same, I don't want Rosie used in that way – and yes, I realise what a huge hypocrite that makes me.

"You know he's a player?" The words leave my mouth before I can stop myself.

"What? What do you mean?"

She stares straight at me as she grips the doorframe with her hand, and I notice that her light pink manicured nails match the colour of her lip-gloss.

"Just be careful. I don't want you to get hurt."

I wonder if I'm being unfairly negative towards Tom and it's more to do with the fact that I don't want Rosie to go on this stupid date or indeed any date. But it's none of my business so long as her social life doesn't interfere with looking after Toby and since she'd asked for the night off, I can't exactly stop her from going out.

"Okay, well, I'd better get going. I'll see you in the morning if you've gone to bed by the time I get back."

I can only nod because any words are stuck in my throat, as if I've swallowed a ton of sawdust which makes the inside of my mouth too dry to speak. She looks nervous, and I hope she's going to change her mind about the date, but then her lips set in a firm line, and she nods back at me before turning and walking out the door. I slump back down onto the sofa and swear under my breath. A fiery jealousy burns through my body even though it hasn't any right to, because I have no say in Rosie's life.

I imagine her laughing and flirting with the jerk, or worse, sleeping with him. I resolve that if he so much as touches a hair on her head, I'll do something painful to his balls – and that thought makes me feel slightly better. I'm still restless though, TV channel hopping all evening and unable to concentrate on anything. I keep glancing at my phone, willing Rosie to message asking me for an excuse to leave the restaurant because her date's a bore, but my phone remains stubbornly silent.

In my head, I replay the evening of the BBQ when Rosie had whirled Toby and Olly around to the beats of Abba playing in the background. They were giggling and singing, and Rosie's face had lit up with sunshine and happiness. Then her eyes caught mine, and I'd been overcome with regret, because I knew I couldn't be the one to love her. I'd loved Sara, but my love wasn't good enough. I won't risk loving someone else again. Love is for dreamers and optimists and I'm neither of those things.

***

The slow, monotonous evening drones on and increases my irritability and heavy black mood. Then, after what seems an eternity, I hear a key in the front door, and I rush out into the hall to see Rosie coming in.

"Are you okay? It's only 10 o'clock," I say, looking at her carefully to check she's all right.

"Yeah, I'm fine." She kicks off her espadrilles and walks barefoot into the kitchen, flicking the switch on the kettle. "Do you want a drink?"

"Uh - yeah, sure, I'll make it."

Rosie nods and goes over to one of the wingback chairs and slumps down, while I quickly make us both mugs of the strong tea she likes and carry them over. Her eyes are closed as she sips the hot amber liquid, and I resist the temptation to ask again if she's okay because it's pretty obvious she's not.

After a minute, she opens one eye and looks at me through her long lashes. "You were right. He is a player." She sits up in the chair and smiles weakly at me. "We hadn't even got through the first course before he was eyeing up the waitress and blatantly flirting with her. I obviously wasn't entertaining enough." She sighs heavily.

"Oh no, I'm sorry." I frown, my mind fast-tracking to all the painful things I'd like to do to the guy.

"It's okay. I suppose it's back to the drawing board." She sighs again but looks slightly more cheerful.

"You're beautiful and funny and smart… I'm sure you'll find the perfect boyfriend soon." I watch as colour travels up her neck and onto her cheeks. Her eyes are intense and a deeper shade of blue tonight, and they focus on mine as she slowly scrapes her hand down her face where it hovers over her collarbone.

I cough into my hand and clear my throat. There's so much I'm tempted to say, but I'm torn with indecision. If I tell her how I feel, there'll be no going back, but I can't offer her a proper relationship. She deserves someone who will always put her above the sun, the moon and the stars. Someone who isn't broken like me.

Chapter 35 – Rosie

He gives out a strangled cry, and he's sick… ALL OVER ME

Matt's been distant all week, and I don't know why. He's polite and chatty whenever Toby's in the room, but it feels like he's avoiding me the rest of the time, locking himself away in his office whenever we're alone in the house. Usually, when Toby's asleep, we spend our evenings together, watching a film or chatting over a glass of wine, but the last three nights he's been out until late, not returning until I've gone to bed. Maybe he's hooked up with someone new after Belle. After all, I reason with myself, an attractive man like him won't remain single for long. Of course, it's none of my business what he gets up to, though I can't help feeling sad that he's turned into Mr Moody again, because I miss the easy banter we used to have.

I've spent the morning catching up with Janine and Caz at the café in the village, and we eagerly listen as Janine shares the latest news about her blossoming love life with Liam.

She's happy and loved up and I can't help feeling a little envious though, after my disastrous date with Tom, I've no desire to do anymore dating myself for a while. I wonder what it must feel like to be wholeheartedly loved and the most important person in someone's world. I've never had that, and maybe I never will.

Abruptly my phone pings with a message from school saying Toby's feeling unwell. Just as I'm reading the message, my phone rings. It's the school secretary telling me several children have come down with a sickness bug, and Toby's just been sick. I need to collect him immediately. I leave Janine and Caz and hastily make my way over to the school reception where Toby's waiting for me. He looks so small and pale and his dark eyes pool with tears as I take his hand.

"It's okay, sweetie. Let's get you home," I smile reassuringly at him.

I sign out his name in the sickness book, and we hurriedly make our way to my car. Toby looks miserable and complains of tummy ache, as he sits in the backseat clutching a plastic bag (which is the only thing I have in the car), in case he has to throw up while we're driving.

Thankfully, we make it home without mishap. I grab a large plastic bowl from the kitchen (more suitable for him to be sick in) and take him straight upstairs to his bedroom. Just as I'm kneeling to help him take off his school uniform, he gives out a strangled cry, and he's sick... ALL OVER ME, missing the bowl completely.

"It's okay, honey. Don't worry." I snatch a towel from the bathroom and wipe up the mess from me and him as best I can. He looks wretchedly at me and is promptly sick again.

"Right, let's get you out of these clothes, and I'll ring your dad." I quickly find him some clean pyjamas and change my own stained top, though I can't do much about the sticky mess in my hair.

I hold Toby in my arms as he whimpers softly into my shoulder, his little face a picture of misery. "Hi, Harry, I'm trying to get hold of Matt, but he's not answering his phone. I think it's switched off." I try to keep my voice steady and calm as Toby nuzzles against me.

"He's out riding with a client. I guess he hasn't got a signal, but he should be back shortly. Is there something I can help with?" Harry's cheerful voice booms down the line.

"No–yes–well, it's Toby. I've just collected him from school, because he's not feeling well. He's just been sick, and I thought Matt would want to know," I rush out.

"I'll try to find him. I expect he'll come straight home." Harry reassures me, and I feel better knowing that Matt will be on his way at any moment.

Chapter 36 – Matt

It's not gentlemanly to throw up on a lady, buddy…

I walk into Toby's bedroom, taking in the chaotic scene. There's a pile of dirty clothes wrapped in towels on the bathroom floor and a large plastic bowl, which usually lives in the kitchen, sits on the bedside table. Toby's legs splay out on either side of Rosie's lap, and he's burrowed his head into her top. He's clearly feeling sorry for himself. I ruffle his hair gently, and Rosie shifts position so I can sit next to her on the bed.

"Why don't I take him now so you can get cleaned up?" I suggest.

Rosie nods gratefully, and we swap places and do an awkward hand-over of Toby. As she exits the bedroom, she leaves an unpleasant trail of vomit odour in her wake. "It's not gentlemanly to throw up on a lady, buddy," I joke. "Let's get you cleaned up and then into bed."

After showering, Toby seems a little better, and he snuggles under his duvet, his eyelids heavy and almost closed, ready for sleep. I leave his door ajar, so I can hear him if he wakes, and make my way downstairs.

***

I've been avoiding Rosie all week, hanging out with Harry at the pub or at his place. It had felt necessary, like self-preservation, to put some distance between us to protect myself from feelings I shouldn't have. But tonight, it feels more like childish behaviour. Rosie's been nothing but her usual sunny self and, to top it all, she's had to deal with Toby puking all over her. I resolve to make it up to her and sharing some Chinese food seems a good start.

Rosie comes into the kitchen a little while later. She's showered and her hair's still damp with the fresh scent of coconut floating in the air around her. Her face is bare of makeup, her nose sun freckled and brown. She's wearing clean dark jeans and a loose fitting off the shoulder white top, and I don't think she's ever looked more beautiful.

"Sorry, Toby threw up all over you. That really was above and beyond your nanny duties."

"Ha, no problem. I've just popped my head around his door, and he's fast asleep."

"Yeah, I think he just needs to sleep it off. Hopefully, he'll feel better when he wakes up. I've ordered Chinese food – hope that's okay? I wasn't sure what you liked, so I've ordered a selection."

"That sounds perfect. I'm starving actually."

I pour us large glasses of chilled white wine, and the food arrives soon after. Delicious smells of garlic, ginger and soy sauce mingle in the kitchen, as I open the various food cartons and lay them out on the table, so we can help ourselves.

"This is so good." Rosie crams more food into her mouth, clearly relishing the Dim Sum, Peking duck and noodles.

"It's refreshing to see someone enjoy their food." I can't help thinking of Belle's penchant for skipping meals and sparrow-like appetite.

"Oh, I love food. It takes lots of calories to maintain this rounded behind."

Rosie laughs, and I wonder if she's flirting with me and if it's appropriate to say how much I love her shapely behind, but then I think better of it. I certainly don't want to risk creating any awkwardness between us tonight.

"Well, I'm glad you're enjoying it, and thanks again for rescuing Toby today." I raise my wine glass to hers, unable to tear my eyes away from her perfectly plump lips...lips that are asking to be kissed.

"So – umm – talking of Belle...are you two definitely over?" Rosie peeks up at me through her dark lashes and bites down on her lower lip.

Of course, she doesn't know that Belle and I weren't together. I wonder why she's looking so nervous. Surely, she doesn't care.

"Yes, we're over. Actually, we've been over for a while and she was only staying here as a favour, because her builder hadn't finished the renovations on her flat." I scrutinise her face, trying to gauge her reaction.

"Really?" Her eyes widen in comprehension as if she's found a lost jigsaw piece and now realises where all the missing parts of the puzzle fit.

I sweep my eyes to hers, holding her intense gaze. "Yes, really. I was just trying to be a good friend, but I should never have let her stay here, and I'm sorry she was so horrible to you."

Rosie's lips turn up into a dazzling smile, and in that instant, I realise that there's a small chance she does indeed care. But what does that mean, because the truth is I've got absolutely nothing to offer her.

***

Before turning in for the night, I check in on Toby to make sure he's okay. He's sleeping peacefully; his fair hair flopped over his serene face. He's beautiful and perfect and, despite everything that's happened, I know how lucky I am to have him as my son.

Just as I walk out onto the landing on my way to my bedroom, I hear what sounds suspiciously like someone throwing up. It can't be Toby this time as realisation dawns that it has to be Rosie.

I knock gently on her bedroom door, but there's only the sound of retching coming from the inside. I brace myself, turning the doorknob and walk in. Rosie's hugging the toilet in her ensuite as another bout of vomiting overcomes her.

"Go away," she mutters as I walk towards her.

"Let me help you." I gently hold her hair back with my fingers, as she's sick again. When the heaving stops, she slumps against the toilet bowl and I grab a towel and dampen it, offering it to her so she can wipe her face. Her skin is grey and clammy, and her eyes stand out like dark pools in her pale face.

"Do you think you're going to be sick again?" I query, as I crouch down at her level and lightly rub my hand up and down her back, hoping to comfort her.

"No, I don't think so," she mumbles into the towel.

"Then let's get you into bed."

Without waiting for a response, I scoop her up into my arms and carry her over to her bed. I lay her down carefully and pull the duvet over her.

"Thank you," she whispers, as she looks up at me with her eyes half closed.

"Try to sleep," I say tenderly, but she's already turned onto her side, curled up with her eyes closed.

***

It's pitch-black outside, the night at its darkest just before dawn. I've tossed and turned for hours, my mind unable to switch off in case either Toby or Rosie needs me. I finally give in and wander into Toby's room to check he's okay. He's still fast asleep - his breathing gentle and rhythmic - and I rearrange his duvet, ensuring his favourite cuddly toy is within easy reach in case he needs it.

Back on the landing, I notice Rosie's light's on, the soft glow escaping from underneath the door, so I knock gingerly, hoping she's all right.

"Come in, Matt."

Rosie's sitting up in bed, her forehead creased in what looks like pain. "Are you okay? Do you need anything?" I stand just inside the doorway, hesitating in case she thinks I'm overstepping, but she gestures me into her room.

"I've woken up with stomach-ache, but I don't feel sick anymore, so at least that's something, I suppose." She gives me a weak smile as another bout of discomfort tightens her face.

"Well, maybe a sip of water will help." I fill a tumbler in the bathroom and return it to her.

"Thanks." She gently pats the side of her bed, inviting me to sit as she takes a few sips of water and then hands the glass back to me.

"Sorry if I woke you. I..." She looks at me, worry etched across her blue irises.

"I was already awake," I cut in, giving her a reassuring smile, as more pain tenses her features.

"Why does everything seem so much worse at night?" There's a sudden, unexpected wobble to her voice.

She looks so dejected and fragile, her golden hair splayed out against the pillow she's leaning against, and all I want to do is pull her into my arms and comfort her. I want to, but I fight the impulse because it isn't my place. "Oh love, I promise you'll feel much better in the morning."

"I..." She suddenly lets out an involuntary sob. "You'll think I'm such a wuss..."

"Rosie?"

"I just... Please don't go." Her eyes are brimming with tears, and then colour reddens her cheeks. "I'm sorry, I... I shouldn't have said that."

Concern tightens my chest; I can't bear to see her upset like this. "Hey," I pull her small hand into mine and squeeze gently. "I won't go anywhere, I promise. Well, maybe just downstairs to make you a hot water bottle or I can rub your back, if it helps?"

"A back rub would be nice."

She turns onto her side, and I begin lightly massaging her back in a small circular motion. Within moments she's asleep, her body finally relaxed and free from tension. Trying not to wake her, I ease myself carefully off her bed and sink into the chair next to it. It's much too small, but I've promised to stay, so that's what I'll do. I get as comfortable as I can, just as the first light of dawn blazons across the fields outside the window.

Chapter 37 - Rosie

Are you propositioning me, Rosie?

I open my eyes and peek at Matt dozing in the chair next to my bed. His hair's messy, as if he's been running his hands through it all night, and he's unshaven; dark stubble growth covering his chiselled jaw and tiredness casting heavy shadows below his closed eyes. He looks uncomfortable, his long legs scrunched up awkwardly; his large frame too big for the small chair he's squeezed into.

I stretch out in bed trying to shake off my sleepiness. I've got a sickness bug, but there's nothing wrong with my eyes, as I take in the beauty of him in his rumpled, dishevelled state. Matt opens his eyes and looks over at me, his perceptive gaze making me feel self-conscious, as if he knows I've been staring at him.

"Good morning." His voice is deep and gravelly from lack of sleep.

"Hi." I smile back at him as I sit up in bed, propping my head against the pillows.

An image suddenly pops into my head of Matt, holding my hair back while I'd thrown up. Then, I remember waking in the night with stomach-ache and getting upset. He's been nothing but kind taking care of me, but I grimace with shame that he's seen me like that.

"Thanks so much for looking after me last night." I take a calming breath, trying to shake off my embarrassment.

"No problem. How are you feeling now?" He sits up in the chair and rests his elbows on his thighs as he looks at me.

"Better, I think. How's Toby?"

"I checked on him earlier and he was still asleep. I thought I'd let him lie-in this morning. He can't go back to school for 48 hours, so there's no reason to wake him."

"I'm sorry I got so emotional. I don't know what came over me, but it was kind of you to stay. Umm…do you want to go to bed?"

Matt's lips twitch into a grin and he quirks an eyebrow. "Are you propositioning me, Rosie?"

"What? Oh no, of course not. No, I just meant you must feel exhausted after taking care of both of us all night. So if you want to catch up on your sleep …." I trail off feeling mortified, as he flings his head back, laughing.

"I was only joking. But if you're feeling okay, I could do with a hot shower and some strong coffee."

While he's unfurling his large body from the chair, I notice my sketch book lying open on the small table at the side. My sketches of Matt and Toby. There's one of Matt looking grumpy labelled 'Mr Moody' and another of him smiling and relaxed labelled 'Mr Gorgeous'. The final one is of the two of them, the day we went on a tour of the stables. Matt's holding Toby in his strong arms, as Toby gently fondles Thunder's forelock. I was desperate to capture such a tender moment, and I've simply labelled it 'Father and Son'.

He notices my horrified expression as I stare transfixed at the open sketch book. Could this day get any worse?

"It was open at this page, but I promise I haven't looked at any other sketches." He tries to reassure me.

"Oh God, I'm so sorry,"

"What on earth for? These sketches are amazing."

"I mean about the labels – you must think I'm incredibly rude."

Matt smirks, his dark eyes dancing with amusement. "I'm sure you could have said a lot worse. I'll take 'moody' and 'gorgeous' over more unflattering descriptions."

I know he's trying to make me feel better, but in the last twelve hours, he's seen me at my worst and most vulnerable. Not only have I thrown up in front of him, but my sketches weren't ever meant to be seen by him. I feel shy and exposed, because I realise he's probably worked out by now that I have feelings for him. Perhaps he senses my discomfort because he smiles uncertainly at me and then walks out of my room, closing the door quietly behind him.

Chapter 38 – Matt

It's my brother's birthday today…

All week Rosie's been distant and quiet towards me, our easy banter replaced with awkwardness after she realised I'd seen her sketches. The book was open, so it wasn't as though I was being deliberately nosy, but maybe I should have closed it before she woke up. I'm actually blown away by her genius at capturing likeness, but rather than being rightly proud of her talent she seems embarrassed I've seen them. I guess it's ironic that I'd spent a week avoiding her company, and now she's doing exactly the same to me.

I've been spending most days at the centre as there's little point being home if Rosie feels uncomfortable around me. However, after a constant stream of interruptions, I decide to head back to the house so I can concentrate on the mountain of invoices that need checking. Hopefully, my home office will be a lot more peaceful.

It's just after 9.30 a.m. and scattered across the azure sky are light cumulus clouds, promising another warm day of sunshine. I open the front door and head towards the kitchen so I can make myself an espresso. There's no sign of Rosie but I switch on the kettle anyway, deciding to make her a mug of her beloved builder's tea, in the hope we can share a drink together before I focus on the dull tasks ahead of me.

The glass doors are open onto the garden, and I realise that Rosie's huddled over the patio table, her shoulders heaving as great ugly sobs wrack her body. She's rocking backwards and forward as she cries uncontrollably.

What the hell! I feel like a voyeur as I continue to observe her and debate what to do. She clearly believes she's alone, but I can't just leave now that I've seen her in so much distress. I walk out onto the patio and gently wrap my arms around her shoulders as her frenzied sobs continue. But she stiffens at my touch, so I let go and instead sit down next to her.

"Hey, Rosie?" But the flow of her tears is out of control, so I decide to wait patiently until she can tell me what on earth has happened, to make her so upset.

After a few moments, she sniffs hard and looks over at me. "I'm okay. Please go away," she mumbles.

"I can't do that. And plainly, you're not okay."

"Honestly, I'm...." Another sob escapes her, and she squeezes her eyes shut and shudders as she tries to catch her uneven breath.

"I'm a good listener. How about I make us both a drink, and you can tell me what the matter is?" I leave her at the table and when I return with tissues and drinks, she's more in control though still inhaling fast shaky breaths, her eyes red raw and puffy.

"You're a really ugly crier." I try to make a joke as I hand her a mug of strong tea.

My reward is a fleeting watery smile, as she takes the tissue I'm offering and blows her nose. I sip my strong espresso, letting the intense caffeine work its magic in my bloodstream, and wait for some kind of explanation.

"It's my brother's birthday today," Rosie finally whispers, her voice wobbly from all the crying. She looks away into the distance as if she can somehow conjure up her brother's image in the fields beyond the garden.

"How old is he?"

"He would have been 32." Another shaky breath and a single fat tear slides slowly down her face.

"Would have been?" Trepidation clings to the pit of my stomach as I wait for what she'll say next.

"He was serving in Afghanistan 10 years ago, and he died."

"Oh God, I'm so sorry."

"It's... it's just because it's his birthday, you know." She sniffles and blows her nose again.

"Do you mind me asking what happened?"

She takes a shaky breath. "He was out on patrol in Helmand Province, and his vehicle was caught in a blast from an IED. They flew him home, but his injuries were too severe. There was nothing they could do." Her tone is monochrome, flat and matter of fact.

I can't think what on earth to say. A momentary shadow falls across the table as the sun slips behind a cloud, and my heart breaks for her. "Tell me about him. I mean, if you'd like to."

She drags her eyes away from the distance and looks at me. "He was 6 years older than me. I was his annoying little sister - he'd grumble I was a pain in his butt and I was. But I could wrap him around my little finger, and I simply adored him. He had dyslexia, and he struggled at school, but he was practical and could repair anything. When he joined up, he became a mechanic, and he found his tribe and what he wanted to do. He loved the army…"

Rosie pauses and takes another shaky breath. "When he died, mum sort of gave up. She'd always had poor health, but it was like she didn't want to live anymore. She just couldn't get over what happened."

She takes a sip of tea and gives me a weak smile. "He'd just got engaged. We were so excited. They were going to set a date for the wedding when he got back."

"Do you still keep in touch with his fiancée?"

"I tried to for a couple of years, but she needed to move on and, I suppose, I was a reminder of the past. She's married now and has a family."

Rosie gazes back over at the distant fields, and I want nothing more than to hold and comfort her. "Where's he buried?"

"Near Oxford."

"Listen, you could go to see him if you want? I'll take you there."   I wonder if I'm being inappropriate, but I've said it now.

"What? I couldn't ask you to do that."

"You're not asking, I'm offering - I'd like to."

"Why?" Her mouth trembles as she worries her bottom lip with her teeth.

"Because I'd like to think we're friends, and that's what a friend would do."

Indecision shows on her face, and the sombre beat of silence drums between us as I wait for her to make her mind up. Finally, she nods. "Thank you," she whispers softly.

"Give me 15 minutes to make a couple of calls - and you really should wash your face." I grin at her, and she returns her first genuine smile since I arrived home an hour ago.

Chapter 39 – Matt

I raged at the world…

A wide, tarmacked driveway sweeps its way upwards into the distance. There are rows of graves on either side, but these are older headstones, most crumbling with decay. They're like lines of decrepit old people, their weary backs bent in defeat because life for them is over. We continue walking up the slight incline to the highest point of the cemetery, and then Rosie turns left towards a newer section. These headstones are black or grey granite with either gold or white lettering which stand out against the dark green of the evergreen trees that edge the boundary of the cemetery. She stops halfway along a row, and I read the headstone.

Sapper Richard James Anderson
25.5.1991-16.1.2013
Corps of Royal Engineers
'He had the heart of a lion'

"I'll sit over there," I say, pointing to a wooden bench a short distance away, though far enough that Rosie hopefully won't feel I'm intruding on her privacy. "Take as much time as you want. We have all day." I smile, trying to reassure her.

Rosie kneels on the neatly mown grass border beside her brother's headstone and, from my vantage point, I'm aware that she's speaking, though I can't make out any of her words. I'm annoyed with myself that I didn't stop on the way to buy flowers, and idly wonder what she's saying to her brother. Maybe she's reminiscing about their childhood together.

The small plaque on my bench reads: 'Sit awhile and be at peace'. It's certainly a tranquil place here – well, I suppose all cemeteries are – and I relax into the quietness; the only interruption are the birds who are feverishly busy with their day. Thankfully, I have a strong phone signal, so, after a while, I reply to a few work emails and check-in with Harry at the yard. I keep a careful eye on Rosie though and, after an hour or so, she stands up and brushes some cut grass from her jeans before making her way towards me.

I rise slowly from the bench as she comes up to me, and I'm taken by surprise as she literally collapses into me. Instinctively, I wrap my arms protectively around her, holding her tightly against my chest, and gently stroke my hand up and down her back in a soothing motion. We stay like that for several minutes before she finally pulls away, and it seems the most natural thing in the world to link my fingers with hers as we sit back down on the bench. Rosie's face is unreadable as she gazes towards her brother's grave but, after a moment, she begins softly speaking.

"When Rich died, I raged at the world. I raged at the person in Afghanistan who planted the IED device that killed him. I raged at the government for sending him there in the first place. I even raged at Rich for wanting to be in the army and being stupid enough to get himself killed. But most of all, I raged at myself because I couldn't be there for him, like he'd been there for me throughout my childhood. He was more than my brother, you see. He was a father figure and someone I looked up to.

"I was angry at God, too. Why had he allowed Rich to die when mum and I had prayed so hard for him to live? But even then, I'd known that, while we were pleading with our God to save Rich's life, there was an Afghan family praying equally hard to their God to save their beloved son and brother, too. And their prayers were just as valid and doubtless just as futile as ours. In that quiet hospital chapel, as dawn broke on the day Rich lost his life, I also realised something else. Why us became, why *not* us. Nothing about war is fair or just, and I was as devastated for that bereaved family in Afghanistan as I was for my own.

"I didn't think I'd ever be able to let go of my anger, but then I slowly realised that I couldn't live my life like that, eaten up with hate and resentment. I can't change what's happened no matter how much I want to but, instead of being bitter because Rich is gone, I try to be grateful he lived, and he was my amazing brother. Life will never be the same, but mostly I'm okay. It's just sometimes, like today, it's harder to be okay."

"I'm so sorry," silently, I groan. I'm used to well-meaning people giving me placatory expressions of sympathy over Sara, and I despise that I'm now doing the same to Rosie.

Reaching over, I hold her gently against me and her body relaxes into me, as the blue cloudless sky wraps calming warmth around us.

"I'm incredibly proud of Rich, and the sacrifice he made for his country. He believed going to Afghanistan was the right thing to do, and perhaps it was. But - I don't know - I can't help questioning the utter waste of it all. Not just Rich's death, but all the other fatalities, too. They were all sons and brothers and husbands, with lives meant for living, not dying." Rosie shifts position slightly, and her eyes find mine.

"I wish I'd had the privilege of knowing him." I squeeze our fingers together lightly.

"You'd have liked him... everyone did. He loved animals - he was always nagging mum for a dog when he lived at home. When she wouldn't get one, he set up his own dog walking business in the village, before and after school. It was quite successful too. He'd dog walk for people who were too busy, and there were a couple of old chaps who couldn't walk far. Then he used the money he made to pay for the occasional riding lesson. He said horses and dogs were kind and had more heart than people did."

"He was right. Horses are therapeutic to be around. They're loyal and never judge you. You didn't share your brother's riding bug then?" I quirk a smile at her.

"Well, no, obviously not." Rosie laughs, probably remembering back to her riding lesson with me. "I didn't have the money, but also I was more the bookworm of the family. I always wanted to do a business degree or study accountancy. Something like that."

"You could still study part time. What about the college that Janine and Liam go to - they'll have courses?"

"I don't know, maybe one day."

I drop my focus down to stare at her short pink nails, which are still threaded through my fingers. Through my peripheral vision, I'm aware of her eyes on our linked hands too, but she makes no move to separate them and neither do I. We sit in contemplative silence, listening to the sounds of vibrant bird life all around us and watch grey squirrels chasing each other through the gravestones with no respect for the dead buried deep within the rich earth below. Dark, intrusive thoughts invade my head space, as I reflect on the pointlessness of Sara and Richard's deaths. I brace myself as the familiar, unbearably raw pain squeezes my chest and the unfathomable question of why they both died loops over and over in my mind.

Chapter 40 – Rosie

Help me heal this beautiful, hurting man…

"You need to forgive yourself, Matt," I say quietly.

Matt stares off into the distance and when he speaks; his voice is barely above a whisper. "I don't think I can."

He looks so lost and sad, and I feel guilty that, by bringing me here, I've made his grief harder to bear. I know he feels torn apart by Sara's death, and there's certainly no time limit on mourning, but he can't seem to let go of the enormous guilt he feels. Of course, I have no right to say anything, but our loss isn't so different, and maybe he'll listen to me.

"Whatever the reasons you feel such guilt about Sara's death, you can't give up on living your life because Sara didn't get to live hers. She made a terrible mistake and paid for it with her life. But thank God Toby wasn't in the car when she was drunk driving. And maybe she'd have eventually realised that being a mum to Toby was more important than being with her boyfriend…or maybe not. Some marriages end, Matt, and it's really sad when it happens, but you're a wonderful father, and Toby's the luckiest boy in the world to have you."

I stop talking, worried I've said too much but, as if he's read my mind, he squeezes my hand in reassurance, and it gives me courage to continue.

"After Rich died, I promised myself I'd live my life in honour of him. To be a person worthy of the sacrifice he made. I vowed I wouldn't waste my life and the opportunities I'm given, and I intend to keep that promise. Don't give up on your own chance of happiness because you think you have to somehow pay for Sara's death."

When he doesn't reply, I sneak a look at him. He's staring off into the distance, his dark eyes pooled with unshed tears. A lone robin hops onto a nearby gravestone and watches us closely before flying off. After a minute, Matt clears his throat and refocuses on me.

"Come on, let's get some lunch."

He releases my hand and rises from the bench and then waits for me to do the same. Immediately, I miss the loss of his touch, but then he grabs hold of my hand firmly again, and we begin slowly walking back down the long drive towards the car. As we pass Rich's grave, I send a silent, pleading message to him, wherever he is, to help me heal this beautiful, hurting man I've fallen for.

***

Matt's mood lifts as soon as we drive away from the cemetery and, once again, I admonish myself for allowing my grief to impact on him when he's struggling so hard to deal with his own. Still, I'm grateful he literally dropped everything to drive me to the cemetery to visit Rich, and I hope I can make it up to him in some small way.

The sun is at its highest point as we find an unoccupied table on the wide lawn outside the café, a few hundred metres from Broadway Tower. Matt disappears inside to order our food, and I slip on my sunglasses and idly people watch, eavesdropping snippets of conversation from nearby tables. The café is busy with a mixture of tourists, cyclists, walkers, and retired folk, enjoying the warm summer day and the unparalleled views of the Cotswold parkland. Gradually, I relax as the sombreness of the morning slowly drifts away.

The emotion of the morning has given us both hearty appetites, and we polish off sandwiches with delicious, generous fillings and freshly baked scones with homemade strawberry jam and clotted cream. As if we've agreed a silent pact not to talk about earlier, I decide a little light-hearted teasing might be fun... at Matt's expense, of course.

"What's this I hear about you and big bananas?" I ask Matt, innocently. A little snigger leaves my mouth as I recall Mrs B sharing the banana double entendre the first day we'd had lunch together.

"Excuse me? I've no idea what you mean," but his lips twitch slightly, so he definitely knows. Frustratingly, before I can challenge him further, he gets up to buy us more drinks. I'm not giving up, though, and by the time he's back, I've got another cock-and-bull story lined up.

"See that couple at the next table?" I whisper conspiratorially and slyly avert my eyes to my left, where a middle-aged man and woman are staring intently into each other's eyes. "They're having a secret rendezvous. I overheard her saying her husband's away and…" I pause dramatically for effect, "they're playing footsie under the table.

"And the pair over there…" I nod my head slightly to my right, while Matt follows my gaze to a young couple who are holding hands, "they're on a first date." I sit back with a smug expression on my face.

"How the hell do you know that?" He grins.

I ignore his question, because I'm enjoying myself now. "See the man with the bow tie who's just come out of the café… he's a food inspector."

"Come on, Rosie, you can't possibly know that." But I can tell from his expression, he's bought the line.

"Honestly, he was wearing a food inspector's hat earlier." Matt's eyebrows shoot up into his hairline, and I can't help smirking. "I promise you. He also had a clipboard and a testing kit to check the fluffiness of the scones and the number of sultanas in them." But then a bubble of laughter bursts out of me, spoiling my elaborate lie.

"Okay, you got me, crazy girl. And, FYI, you'd have got away with it, if you hadn't over-embellished with the food inspector guy… scone testing kit indeed!" Matt throws back his head, laughing, and I store the image away in my mind, so I can sketch this relaxed, happy version of him later when we're home.

I also realise that watching Matt laugh is highly addictive, and all I want to do is make it happen again and again. This day may have started out badly but, if I have anything to do with it, it'll end far better.

***

After lunch, we meander past the landmark Broadway Tower on Beacon Hill, taking the stony footpath that leads into fields of skittish red deer and graceful horses standing under heavily shaded trees sheltering from the heat of the early afternoon. Ahead of us are a couple of wooden benches set on a sort of viewing platform and we sit down, taking in the spectacular views of 16 counties in the distance. The view would usually captivate me, but my mind is elsewhere.

Adrenaline races through me, as if I'm high on too much caffeine, and my senses heighten. I'm acutely aware of Matt's nearness, his masculinity, the smell of his aftershave... him. There's anticipation hanging in the air and maybe he feels it too because when our eyes lock, I see uncertainty there, or perhaps he's asking my permission? Trying to read his thoughts, I smile slightly, hoping that's all the reassurance he needs.

"I know this is probably bad timing... I'm really attracted to you, and I think you feel the same." His voice is low and gravelly, sending shivers of excitement through me.

"I feel a 'but' coming." I lift an eyebrow in question.

"But..." he begins - then he leans in, placing the palm of his hand behind my head and gently grazes his lips against mine. His touch is light but firm and, as my mouth falls open, he deepens our kiss, and our tongues begin slowly dancing in exquisite rhythm.

God, I need to remember to breathe. I fist his shirt as if my life depended on it, feeling his hard, heated body through my fingertips. Matt lets out a deep, throaty moan as his kiss becomes more urgent - more demanding - and his hand rakes through my hair, pulling me closer as I surrender myself completely to him.

Even in this perfect moment, I recall there was a 'but' left unsaid. And sure enough, he suddenly pulls away and, like a fleeting whisper, the kiss is over and drifts away in the warm air. Immediately, I feel the absence of his lips on mine, and my stomach clenches in disappointment.

"I'm sorry, I shouldn't have done that." Matt's eyes are dark with regret.

"Why?" I murmur, though I already know his answer.

"Because I don't do proper relationships, Rosie. Not after Sara, anyway. I only do one-night stands and with Belle it was casual hook-ups or, as you so aptly described it, friends with benefits. I don't do love or commitment or anything remotely long term or worthwhile."

I won't be a casual hook up. "I won't—"

But Matt interrupts me. "I wouldn't ask you to. I don't want that with you." His voice is gruff.

"Here comes another but…" I mumble, more to myself than to Matt.

"I can't let go of the past and what happened to Sara. It's broken me. And every time I think about moving on, I hate myself even more." Matt's voice cracks. "As time passes - as the rawness and grief fades little by little - I feel more guilt, not less."

"I can't compete with Sara," I whisper wearily. *How can anyone compete with a dead person?* My shoulders slump in defeat, as this perfect moment between us is over.

"I wouldn't want you to. You're you and you're amazing. And you know the crazy thing – maybe because Sara and I weren't happy, that just makes everything so much worse." He sighs heavily. "It's time we got back." He rises from the bench and offers me his hand, but I swiftly sidestep him, rebuffing it.

A cacophony of conflicting emotion battles in my head. I refuse to be a one-night stand or casual hook-up but, all the same, I can't help feeling hurt by Matt's rejection. And, although I've no right to be, I'm also frustrated that he won't allow himself to move forward with his life. But most of all, I'm upset that things are now back to being awkward between us.

Matt follows me as we make our way back up the hill and once we're in the car, we settle into uncomfortable silence on the drive back. My senses are in overload though: the smell of him - the taste of him - the feel of him. Especially the feel of him and the pressure of his lips on mine as we'd kissed. All of it burnt into my memory. I glance over at Matt and wonder if he's thinking about our kiss too, but his expression is closed off and unreadable.

**

Matt's kiss is still playing on my mind when we stop off to collect Toby from school. Obviously, Matt regretted it, his eyes full of apology, telling me everything. He's not ready to let go of the past and move on, and I need to respect that. There's also nothing to be gained by pining for someone I can't have and sulking about it either. I humph out a sigh, resolving to put Matt and his incredible kiss firmly behind me.

Toby clambers onto the backseat of Matt's car and hands me a note about a forthcoming bake-sale to raise funds for the school. It will take place on Friday and each child is being asked to bring in either bought or home-made cakes to be sold over lunchtime. I paste on a bright 'fake it till you make it' smile, hoping to assuage the awkwardness between us. Perhaps Matt feels the same, because we spend the rest of the journey home in light-hearted debate about which type of cake Toby should bake.

"It's got to be coffee and walnut – it's a classic combination," Matt suggests first.

"Or how about a lemon drizzle cake, Toby? Lemon's so summery and fresh," I counter.

"You can't beat a traditional Victoria sandwich," Matt retorts.

"Or maybe a chocolate cake?" I bat back. "Everyone loves chocolate."

"Carrot cake's always good." Matt gives me a sideways look like he's determined to win the cake argument.

"Ugh, no way! Cinnamon's the devil's food." I look aghast at Matt, and we both wait with bated breath for Toby's verdict.

"I want to make chocolate cupcakes with lots of sprinkles on top," he finally pronounces.

"Yeeess!" I whoop with joy and clap my hands, feeling like I've just won a popularity contest between us. Matt groans but is magnanimous in defeat.

"Good choice, Toby. Make some extra ones for me, won't you?" He looks at Toby in the mirror and laughs.

The cake rivalry is the distraction we both need and, by the time we arrive home, the atmosphere between us is almost back to normal, at least for now.

Chapter 41 – Matt

Sparkling sunshine on the ocean…

"Thanks for taking me to see Rich today and being such a good friend." Rosie looks across at me as I kill the car engine. Toby's out of the car immediately and waiting impatiently for us at the front door to be let in.

"A friend, huh?" I can't help smirking. "I'm sorry about earlier and I'll try to be…um…a better friend, or at least a friend that doesn't kiss you."

The truth is, I don't regret for one moment kissing Rosie, although I can't blame her for being annoyed after I pulled away. She merely nods and I give her, what I hope, is a reassuring smile, before we both get out of the car and go into the house, whereupon Toby races into the kitchen to find snacks.

For the rest of the day, we both try hard to act normally around each other and to put our brief kiss behind us, although, in my case, that's impossible. Once Toby's in bed, I retreat to my office and try to catch up on the accounts work I'd left this morning, but I feel distracted and unsettled, our kiss playing over and over in my head.

I can still feel Rosie's soft lips on mine; the way her breath hitched as our tongues tangled together and her body melted into mine. Her perfume, like sparkling sunshine on the ocean, intoxicated my senses, so all I could think about was my overpowering need for her. I'd wanted her with such fierceness and intensity, yet I'd pulled away and rejected her like the prize idiot I am.

I try to convince myself it's for the best, but whatever my head might think it wants, my heart doesn't agree, and eventually I abandon work altogether and pour myself a whiskey. Sipping the amber liquid slowly, I watch as dusk turns to nightfall, the long eerie shadows falling over my desk as I try to keep my emotions from spinning recklessly out of control.

Rosie said I needed to forgive myself, but I don't know how.

Much later, I go up to bed, but the darkness brings no relief from the turmoil I'm feeling as I toss and turn, unable to sleep until dawn breaks.

Chapter 42 - Rosie

I want to sulk and tantrum like a petulant toddler…

It's raining; a persistent, heavy downpour that looks set in for the day. The slate grey overcast sky matches the gloom of my mood and my head throbs with the supreme effort I'm making to forget Matt's kiss. I sigh heavily. *I remember every single detail.* The way his lips felt on mine, the way his tongue explored mine, the taste of him, the smell of him… him.

He doesn't want me, though. He's made it abundantly clear he's not over Sara's death and he doesn't want another relationship again. Like acid, the harsh sting of disappointment burns my stomach at the memory of his rejection. I want to sulk and tantrum like a petulant toddler at the unfairness of it all. For the hundredth time, I tell myself I'm okay. But as hard as I try to convince myself that I respect Matt's decision, regret, like my deflated mood, remains.

I trudge through the morning - getting Toby to school and doing a big supermarket food shop, including buying ingredients for the chocolate cupcakes he'll be baking tonight. I also consider what Matt said about enrolling on an accountancy or business course at college. While I love being Toby's nanny, that won't last forever, and if I can gain a professional qualification, then there'll be more career openings in the future. I'm seeing Caz and Janine at the community café later and I decide to enquire at the college about courses beforehand to see if it's possible to study part-time while Toby's at school.

***

By the afternoon, the heavy rain has stopped and the dark clouds, like my despondent mood, have finally lifted. Caz and Janine are already at a table in the café and have ordered our drinks and large slabs of sticky ginger cake to go with them.

"Sorry I'm late." I smile in greeting. "I've just been to enquire about courses at the college." Placing the college prospectus on the table, I explain about my potential plan to do an accountancy course, or something similar, as long as it will fit around Toby's school hours.

"That's a great idea. I'm sure Matt would appreciate some help with the centre accounts." Caz smiles encouragingly.

"Oh, I wasn't thinking…" I trail off. The last thing I need is to get more involved in Matt's life. I don't think my emotions can take it. "I'm sure he needs someone far more experienced than me," I reply lamely.

"How are things between you two, anyway? Harry says Matt's finally come to his senses and Belle's history, sooo…?" Caz's inferred question hangs in the air.

"Oh, I haven't seen much of him lately. He's so busy with the centre." The lie leaps out of my mouth as I try to deflect. "How's it going with Liam?" I ask Janine, changing the subject.

"Really well, thanks. Only… he's got us some tickets to see a local band at the pub tonight. I've already told him I can't get a babysitter, but I just wondered…."

"Of course, I'll have Olly. He can help Toby make cakes for the school sale. Can you let me have his overnight bag when I pick them up from school later?"

"Thanks, Rosie. I really owe you. I promise I'll have Toby for a sleepover any time you and Matt have plans." Janine smiles gratefully at me.

"I really don't mind. Olly's no trouble at all and Toby will be super happy," I say, ignoring Janine's little probe about Matt and me. I'm certain they both know I have feelings for him, and I wonder if I should tell them about his kiss, but what would be the point? Matt doesn't want me, so I need to move on with my life and put Matt and his kiss firmly behind me.

Chapter 43 - Rosie

Ugh! It tastes of....

Finally, the two rascals are in bed. It's past 8 p.m. and cake debris, dirty mixing bowls and left over ingredients litter the kitchen table, as I slowly begin clearing up the mess. The boys have had a riot of fun, as evidenced by the carnage, but are now fast asleep after their baking triumph. I glance over at the 24 chocolate cupcakes, decorated generously with buttercream and sprinkles, which sit proudly on display, waiting to be admired by Matt when he returns from the centre.

By the time Matt gets back, the kitchen resembles normality, and the mixing bowls are back in use, as I make more cake batter. I sigh wearily. It's been a long day and I've still got 24 chocolate cupcakes to bake and decorate before I go to bed.

Matt looks admiringly at the boys' cakes, while he pours us both a glass of wine and hands me one. "They look amazing, Rosie. Did Toby have fun?"

"Yes, he did, and Olly did, too. I hope you don't mind, but Janine needed a last-minute babysitter, so I said he could stay over."

Matt smiles at me. "No problem, though I imagine it's been hard work trying to keep them in line with both of them baking." He grabs one of the cakes, but I put my hand up to warn him.

"I wouldn't if I were you," I caution.

"Why?" He looks at me, confused.

"Just taste a bit of the chocolate buttercream." I watch as he scrapes a little onto his finger.

"Ugh! It tastes of–,"

"Salt," I help him out.

"Yeah, that's right, salt." He confirms my diagnosis.

"I didn't notice they'd grabbed the salt caddy instead of the icing sugar one." I confess. "By the time I realised it was too late, and I didn't have the heart to tell them, because they were having so much fun."

Matt looks at my sheepish expression and bursts out laughing. "You mean you let them get away with it?"

"Well, yes, I suppose so. But it was my fault really, because I should have kept a closer eye on what they were doing."

"Knowing the two reprobates upstairs, they were most likely larking about." He continues laughing at me, and I can't help joining in.

"So, by the look of things, I'm guessing you're making another batch of cakes?"

"Yes, well, I thought if I substituted mine for theirs, they'd be none the wiser and no-one would get upset."

"That's sweet of you, though the boys don't deserve it. How about I make us both something to eat while you finish the cakes?"

"That sounds a good plan," I say gratefully. I'd fed the boys when they'd come back from school, but I hadn't eaten anything, and I suddenly realise how hungry I am.

Matt prepares the ingredients for a pasta carbonara and, once the cakes are in the oven, we sit together at the kitchen table eating our food, the pancetta and pecorino cheese mingling with the delicious baking smells.

"I'd have thought the boys would have been eager to try out their cakes. How on earth did you persuade them not to?" Matt peers at me over his wine glass, his amused eyes laughing at me.

"I'm afraid I bribed them with three scoops of chocolate ice-cream and promised they could have a cake each for breakfast. I'll give them fruit as well," I add hastily, hoping that will make up for their unhealthy start to the day.

"Rosie Anderson, what sort of nanny are you?" Matt teases me, but I love the fact we're back to being at ease with each other again.

After dinner, Matt clears away and I start on the second batch of buttercream. Then, together, we decorate the cakes so that they look as haphazard in design as the boys' ones were. By the time we finish, it's late, and a bubbling brook of happiness ripples inside me as I peek at Matt and his dark, mesmerising eyes hold mine, immersing me in their intense depth. Desire, like the currents of an unstoppable tide, flows through me and I catch my breath. I can't think of anywhere I'd rather be or anyone I'd rather be with, and it's clear from Matt's face that he feels the same.

Chapter 44 – Matt

Kiss the ever-loving life out of her…

Desire burns in Rosie's heated eyes and, like a magnetic force field I'm unable to escape from, I stride towards her, pulling her roughly into my arms, and kiss the ever-loving life out of her. Her need matches my own as all rational thought vanishes and we're lost in each other, our lust uncontrollable as our tongues tangle together.

I slip one hand underneath her T-shirt, yanking the lace material of her bra down, and begin rubbing the pad of my thumb gently against her pebbled nipple. A desperate moan of desire escapes from her throat, but I clamp down harder on her mouth and walk her slowly backwards until she bumps into the dresser. She's hitching herself against me, her breath ragged and uneven, as she tugs at the top button on my jeans. Then suddenly she tenses, so I instantly pull away and take a step back.

Chapter 45 – Rosie

F**king annoying man!

I feel Matt's hardness against me as I fumble to unbutton the top of his jeans. I'm frantic with desire, with my overpowering need for him, but then a small persistent voice seeps into my consciousness and cold reality sobers me. I can't do this until I know it's not just a casual hook-up. Matt senses the change because he immediately releases me, and I feel distraught at what's likely to happen next.

"I want you." Matt's voice is gravelly with desire as his molten eyes seize mine.

I look back at him, my heart thumping wildly. "I want you too but…"

"But?" he repeats, as I swallow down hard trying to keep my voice from breaking.

"I can't sleep with you for brief gratification."

The edges of Matt's lips turn up into a smirk. "Well, there won't be any sleeping involved, and it certainly won't be brief."

A heated blush crawls up my neck and onto my cheeks. "You know what I mean. Unless something's changed…?" I leave the question hanging, but I already know his answer.

"Nothing's changed," he murmurs, his voice so low I can hardly hear him.

"Then I'm sorry. I'm sure lots of women would live in the moment, but that's just not me."

Matt doesn't say anything but there's conflict in his face – a battle of his desire for me over giving in to my demand for something more than a one-night stand. Undoubtedly, the same emotions are reflected in my expression. I scoot away from his reach, my stomach a painful vice of hurt, clamping down on me so I can barely breathe.

By the time I reach my room, I've used up every swear word I know courtesy of my brother's army potty mouth. F**king annoying man!

Chapter 46 – Matt

I finally reach a decision…

What the hell was I thinking?

I sit at the kitchen table, head in my hands, trying to make sense of what's just happened. All my resolve to keep Rosie at a distance had flown out the window, and I hadn't wanted to think about anything but kissing her, possessing her, making her mine. I'd lost all self-control, and I'd wanted her with a fierce intensity that had overwhelmed me.

Then she'd pulled away and asked me if I'd changed my mind about having a relationship with her. I'd wanted with all my heart to say yes, but then gut-wrenching guilt rose like bile in my throat and made me hesitate. Instantly, disappointment engulfed her face, and she'd turned away, leaving me with a chasm of regret of my own making.

Now, as I sit in the fading light, I think back over the last four years since Sara died and I finally reach a decision. But before I tell Rosie, I need to do something first.

Chapter 47 – Rosie

It's becoming a habit…

I've dropped the boys off at school, each proudly carrying a tray of cakes that look as slapdash and messy as theirs had been. I congratulate myself that they're none the wiser, and my little deception has worked. It was definitely worth it to see their excitement this morning. And, as promised, they each had a cake for breakfast, together with a dish of strawberries, blueberries and banana.

Matt had already left for the stables by the time the boys and I were up. But, as I walk into the kitchen, he's back and sitting at the table sipping the bitter, unpalatable drink he likes to call coffee.

"I'm sorry. I crossed the line last night," he says without preamble.

"It's becoming a habit." I can't help smiling. "Anyway, it wasn't just you. We both crossed the line."

Matt smiles back apologetically. "Yes, well, it was wrong of me."

"You need to make up your mind about what you want, Matt." An unintended note of frustration edges into my voice and pent-up exasperation knots my stomach, but he pointedly ignores me and changes the subject.

"Anyway, we're invited to Harry's birthday dinner tomorrow night. Are you up for it?"

"Together, you mean?" I look at him, confusion in my eyes.

"Well, I'll be there, and you'll be there, so yes, I guess we'll be together." He raises his eyebrow at me and grins.

"I'm definitely up for it." I laugh and butterflies start flip-flopping in my tummy in anticipation of what tomorrow night might bring.

Chapter 48 – Matt

It's time I let you go…

"I've bought your favourite flowers," I say to the air around Sara's gravestone. Crouching down, I arrange the yellow sunflowers over her grave, awkwardness sweeping over me. I've never been a frequent visitor, and it feels like the occupants of nearby graves are silently passing judgment on me for staying away for so long.

"I want to say…" I stop. It feels ridiculous talking to a gravestone when I'm pretty sure Sara can't hear me. My resolve trickles away, but then I remember Rosie sitting next to her brother's grave talking to him, so I press on.

"Toby will be seven soon and you've missed so much of his growing up already. He's doing really well at school, and he's just started learning to ride. I tell him how amazing you were, and I promise I'm trying to be the best father I can."

An elderly woman is busy cleaning a gravestone further along the row. I wonder if it's her husband's grave. She's kneeling, intent on her task, and I watch her for a few moments, trying to think of the next words I want to say.

"I regret so many things that happened, but not that I fell in love with you, and we made Toby together. Our marriage – well, we can both agree it wasn't perfect, but I'll always be grateful you were my first love, Sara."

I watch the old lady some more. She's arranging her own flowers now. Pink roses, but not the long-stemmed ones you buy. These look home-grown - a higgledy-piggledy array of blooms from a garden. I wonder if they're for a birthday or an anniversary.

"I miss you, and I wish with all my heart that things had been different, and you hadn't died."

A soft, low murmur, like a gentle whisper, drifts over. The old lady appears to be speaking to her gravestone, too.

"I'm so sorry for everything that happened. I'm sorry for the hurt and the anger we caused each other. I'm sorry for all of it."

She's also having a one-sided tête-à-tête, but she seems far more at ease doing it than I am. Maybe she's done it before.

"I'll always remember the laughter and the good times we had together. I'll always remember how much I loved you."

She's ceased talking now, but she hasn't moved. I watch as she takes out a tissue from her pocket and dabs her eyes. I wonder who she's weeping for.

"You'll always be my beautiful Sara, but it's time I let you go, my darling girl." I get up and slowly step back from Sara's grave. "Sweet dreams, my love."

I blow a soft kiss into the still air and begin walking away, my face damp with silent tears. But there's also an unfamiliar sense of peace within me.

I glance over to the grave where the old lady had been, but she's no longer there.

Chapter 49 – Rosie

I let myself pretend that we really are a couple…

"Happy Birthday, old man." Matt slaps Harry on the back and hands him a bottle of Jameson Black Barrel whiskey.

Harry laughs. "Look who's calling me old. I'm more like a fine wine, aged to perfection."

"Or smelly old vintage cheese." Caz joins in, laughing. "Dinner won't be long, but let's open the wine and have a birthday toast." She hands us each a glass of red, and we all clink glasses.

I sip my wine slowly, appreciating its richness and flavour, and listen to the easy camaraderie between Harry and Matt as they continue to banter and tease each other mercilessly.

Matt's happy and relaxed, but it feels much more than that, though I can't quite put my finger on why. It's like something within him has shifted. His whole demeanour seems lighter and more carefree somehow. Matt's lemony aftershave floats in the air and mingles with his clean, masculine smell. The combination is heady and delicious; his nearness making me almost lightheaded with need. My eyes drift to the contour of his chest through his white shirt, and I want to shamelessly reach out and touch him. Warmth heats my cheeks as I remember his hard body against mine and how he'd held me possessively in his arms as we'd kissed.

While I'm lost in thought, Matt suddenly turns and looks expectantly at me, but I haven't been listening to the conversation.

"You haven't any idea what we've just been saying, have you?" His eyebrow lifts in that sexy way he does as he drapes his arm over the back of my chair.

"Umm, no sorry, I was just having a moment. This wine's lovely. It's so nice to relax after a busy day."

"Where's Toby tonight?" Harry asks me.

"He's having a sleepover with Olly. He's been looking forward to it all day, and he'd packed his overnight bag by 10 this morning. I just hope they actually get some sleep tonight, otherwise poor Janine will be exhausted."

Caz brings in a casserole and serves us big helpings of Coq au vin, which smells heavenly of chicken, rich red wine, onions, garlic and mushrooms. There's also bowls of crisp roast potatoes and French beans.

"This tastes amazing." I smile at Caz.

"Here's to the chef." Matt toasts, and we all clink glasses again.

After dinner and a riotous rendition of 'happy birthday' to Harry, we play charades; our guesses becoming more bizarre and funnier as the evening wears on. We abandon the game just as the last of a dazzling, fiery sunset disappears over the fields and darkness falls, altering the mood to a more intimate one. I'm sprawled out next to Matt, and he's nursing a tumbler of his favourite whiskey, while his other arm drapes tantalising close to me across the back of the sofa. It's been the perfect evening and, with Matt almost touching me, I let myself pretend that we really are a couple.

"Anyone for coffee?" Caz asks, tilting her head slightly to show I should follow her into the kitchen. Reluctantly, I get up from the languid comfort of Matt's side and trail after her as she leaves the room.

"You've fallen hard, haven't you?" Caz says softly as she meets my eyes across the kitchen, her lips forming into a worried frown.

"What...what do you mean?" I ask, embarrassment colouring my cheeks.

"You haven't taken your eyes off Matt all evening and...umm...well...I just don't want you to get hurt."

My cheeks are on fire now. They probably match the deep red colour of my top. I wonder if there's any point in trying to deny it, but Caz hasn't finished.

"Look, I probably shouldn't say, but Matt told Harry this morning that Belle's been messaging him."

I nod slowly. Of course, she'd want to get back with him. They make a perfect couple. "Do...do you think he'll get back with her?" I ask quietly. Even though I don't want to know the answer, I'm a sucker for punishment.

"I don't know, but Harry says he's meeting up with her tomorrow 'to talk'." Caz curls her fingers into bunny ears signifying air quotes and sighs, concern in her kind eyes. "Come on, let's forget the coffee and get drunk on Matt's expensive whiskey."

She pulls me to her and gives me a massive hug. My throat tightens and I swallow down hard, trying to hold back the tears which threaten to overwhelm me. How could I have been so stupid to have imagined Matt and me as a couple! Caz gently leads me into the sitting room and pours us both a good measure of whiskey and I gulp it down, feeling its bitterness hit the back of my throat. The sting makes me want to cough, but I swig another large mouthful instead.

Caz sits down next to Harry, but I stay where I am and top up my glass and knock that back too. The heat punches my stomach, but I don't care. I just want to blot out the humiliation of the evening. Then my befuddled brain realises something else. Of course, it would explain why Matt's in such a happy, relaxed mood. I bet he can't wait to make up with Belle and, no doubt, he's feeling embarrassed by my stupid, love-struck behaviour tonight. My hand reaches for the whiskey again, but another bigger hand grips the bottle, and Matt's tall frame towers over me.

"Don't you think you've had enough?" His voice is firm, with an undercurrent of confusion at my sudden change of behaviour. He takes the glass from me, and his fingers brush against mine. It's like an electric shock pulsating through me and brings me to my senses.

"I should go home," I mumble. "Thanks for a lovely evening and delicious meal, Caz, and happy birthday Harry. I… um… I've had a great time. Thank you for inviting me." I move swiftly towards the door, not waiting for Matt, and almost run out into the darkness.

Chapter 50 – Rosie

Lovely lemons…

"What's wrong?" Matt asks me for the second time, as I bound along towards home. Even though his legs are much longer, I'm outpacing him as I scoot along, intent on reaching the refuge of my room as fast as possible and putting an end to this humiliating evening.

I don't answer him. I'm too upset, too embarrassed and, above all, too angry at myself for naively believing that Matt would ever really be interested in me. He was probably just killing time until he and Belle made up. We reach home in record time, and I make straight for the stairs to escape to my room, but Matt's having none of it.

"No, you don't. In here." He points sternly to the sitting room and steers me towards the sofa. "Sit." His voice is firm, brooking no argument.

I sit obediently and close my eyes, attempting to stop my head from spinning. The mix of too much alcohol, the cool night air, and my jangled emotions are making me feel woozy and lightheaded. Matt crouches in front of me and places his arms on either side of my body so that I'm caged in.

"What's the matter?" he asks gently. I slowly open my eyes and see him gazing at me intently. His deep brown eyes hold mine, but I don't want to look at him, so I peer down at my lap.

"Nothing," I whisper, though traitorous tears threaten to betray me.

Matt lightly raises my chin with his finger so I'm back, looking at his penetrating eyes. "Well, that's clearly not true, so I ask again, what's the matter?" His voice is firmer this time. "What exactly did Caz say to you in the kitchen?"

"What do you mean?" I whisper.

"I mean, you went into the kitchen happy, yet when you came out, you were clearly upset about something, and then you slugged down a lot of good whiskey like it was water."

"It wasn't Caz that upset me." I glare at him and poke my finger at his chest in anger. "It was you."

"Me?" Matt asks incredulously, his brows furrowing in confusion.

"Yes!" I glare at him, challenging his beautiful, dark eyes with my own. He continues to stare at me, and I fill in the silence. "It felt strange, that's all."

"What did?"

"Us being there together, like a proper couple, which I know we're not. And I'm sure you'd have preferred spending the evening with Belle. But it's okay, because you'll soon be back together." Through my fog of alcohol, I try to sound reassuring. "I bet you can't wait. I mean, Belle's 6 feet tall and stick thin – she must be a size 6 whereas I'm obviously not. In fact, I don't think I've ever been a size 6, and do you know why not?" I continue to rant and jab him in the chest with my finger.

"I don't, but I'm sure you're going to enlighten me." His voice is full of amusement, as if my outburst is entertaining him, which incenses me even more.

"Because I eat proper food and not green gloopy shakes that have disgusting things in them." I sit back, a self-satisfied look on my face.

"Well, that's very informative." Matt's lips turn up into a smirk, and he gently pulls a strand of my hair behind my ear. "I think you need to go to bed and sleep off the whiskey, and we'll talk properly in the morning once you've sobered up."

"Umm, yes, let's go to bed." I intend to sound seductive, but it comes out more slurry than sexy. I stare brazenly at Matt and watch as he raises his eyebrows in amusement.

In my alcohol haze, I register that he's lifting me effortlessly from the sofa. I wrap my arms around his neck and snuggle into his chest as he carries me upstairs. "You smell lemony," I murmur, "Lovely lemons!" I let my lips gently graze his neck. Then I kiss him there softly… slowly… as I breathe him in. Everything about being in Matt's arms feels right, and I decide I want to stay exactly where I am forever.

"Hmm, well, you smell of strong Irish whiskey, and you're going to have the mother of all hangovers tomorrow." Matt laughs dryly as he places me gently on my bed. I feel lonely the moment his arms leave me, and I desperately want to be back where I belong, but then blackness envelops me, and I fall into a deep dreamless sleep.

Chapter 51 – Matt

I will put this right…

I carefully remove Rosie's sandals and then place her duvet over her. She's sleeping soundly – passed out more like from too much booze – her face tranquil in repose. Her tousled sun-kissed hair is splayed out over her pillow, and I gently remove a stray wisp from her cheek. She looks incredibly beautiful, despite her smudged mascara and flushed face.

From what I've surmised from earlier, Rosie thinks I'm about to get back with Belle, but that's the furthest thing from my mind. And I would have told her that if she hadn't been so inebriated. I groan inwardly at the thought of the massive hangover she's going to have tomorrow.

I keep our bedroom doors slightly ajar so I can hear if she wakes during the night needing to throw up. Then, I lie on my bed, thinking. Tomorrow I will put this right.

Chapter 52 – Rosie

Popping corks from sparkling champagne…

My shrill alarm shocks me awake and I reach over to my bedside table, fumbling to turn it off. Every part of me wants to turn over and go back to sleep. But then snapshots of the evening gradually begin colliding with the biggest thumping headache I've ever had. I cautiously sit up in bed and wait for the room to stop swaying and then gingerly put my feet on the floor, hoping I can remain upright.

It's a relief to realise I'm still wearing my clothes from last night and therefore Matt hadn't undressed me, embarrassment heating my cheeks at the thought. My mouth feels dry like gritty sandpaper, so I tentatively make my way to the bathroom and brush my teeth, but I can't face showering. I need strong builder's tea first and lots of it.

I make my way slowly downstairs to the kitchen and fill the kettle. As I'm waiting for it to boil, I relive the end of Harry's birthday evening and my discovery that Belle had been messaging Matt, and that they're meeting up today to talk. I sigh in resignation, because it's obvious they're thinking of getting back together. I'd been eaten up with jealousy last night, but that was no excuse for the way I'd acted. Just as I'm contemplating crawling back to bed and hiding under my duvet in shame, Matt comes into the kitchen.

"Morning," he greets me cheerfully, but all I can do is groan as I clutch my head in my hands. "Here." He hands me a glass of water and a couple of paracetamol. "This'll help your head."

"I'm so sorry, Matt." Heat burns my cheeks as I feel them turn crimson. "I'm so embarrassed about last night. All the unkind things I said about Belle and the way I behaved with you." Suddenly, I remember kissing Matt's neck and another wave of shame washes over me.

He grins and gives me a mug of strong tea he's made. "It was the whiskey talking, that's all. You were smashed out of your mind on the stuff."

"I really am sorry," I repeat. I wonder what else I can say, as he takes the seat next to mine and regards me thoughtfully.

"Look, about last night. You really shouldn't compare yourself to anyone else, Rosie. You're beautiful and smart and funny and sexy... well, maybe not so sexy right now." He smirks at me.

I grimace. I certainly don't feel sexy at the moment, with my raging hangover, bed hair, and bloodshot eyes.

"What exactly did Caz say to you last night?" His dark eyes hold mine.

I lower my eyes to stare at my tea and wonder if I can get away with not telling him, but I haven't got the energy to lie.

"She said you'd told Harry that Belle's been messaging you, and you're meeting up today to talk." My words come out in a garbled hurry, and a lone tear slowly slides down my cheek at the thought of him getting back with her. And if they are getting back together, will it be a casual thing again, or maybe this time Matt wants more? Not that it matters, of course.

Matt exhales a heavy breath but before he can say anything, I ask my own question, keeping my eyes still carefully fixed on my tea, as I can't bring myself to look at him. "Are you getting back together?" I mumble.

Matt gently tips my head up so that I'm looking directly at him and wipes away my tear with the pad of his thumb. "Maybe you shouldn't always listen to Caz." He pauses. "But yes, Belle's been messaging. And yes, we're meeting up later. She has a horse in livery here, so I imagine it's about moving him to another yard."

"So, you're not getting back together?" I squeak out.

"No, of course we're not getting back together." His voice is gentle, and I see the honesty of his words in his eyes. Relief floods through me, but he hasn't finished. "You said last night that you found it strange us being there together, like a proper couple. But, here's the thing... I want, more than anything, for us to be together. I want a relationship with you, Rosie. A proper committed relationship and I'm sorry it's taken me so long to figure that out and to stop acting like an idiot."

I wonder if the alcohol infused fug in my head has affected my hearing. Did he just say he wanted a committed relationship with me?

"I seem to have fallen for a hungover, opinionated nanny who's incredibly beautiful despite her smudged mascara panda eyes." He brushes his thumb slowly under my eye as another fat tear escapes. "I want you, Rosie Anderson, and I hope with all my heart that you still want me." He stops, and I sense his nervousness. "Do you still want me?" His voice is low and gravelly.

Despite my thumping headache, utter joy is bubbling up inside me at Matt's words, and I want to kiss him so badly. But I need to know something first. "What changed your mind?"

"I kept thinking about what you'd said about forgiving myself. I didn't think I'd ever be able to do that, but then, after I watched you talking to Rich at the cemetery, I wondered if I could somehow make things right with Sara… I don't know, it sounds crazy."

"No, it doesn't. Go on," I encourage him.

"I went to her grave and told her how sorry I was for everything that had happened. Afterwards, I felt a sense of peace, or maybe her forgiveness. Or that I can finally forgive myself. I can't explain it, but now it feels like I'm ready to let Sara go."

"Are you sure?" My voice is barely above a whisper, but I need to know that he's finally ready to move forward with his life.

"Yes, I'm completely sure. I love you, Rosie, and I want us to build a future together." He pauses and there's tension in his eyes. "But you haven't answered my question. Do you still want me?" His mouth sets into a tight frown.

"Of course, I want you." I fling my arms around his neck, emotions exploding inside me, and it's not from my hangover. It's an explosion of love for him, fizzing and bubbling like popping corks from sparkling champagne.

Matt slightly pulls back and places his strong hands on either side of my cheeks. Slowly, his lips graze mine and he kisses me softly, but I can't help tugging at his hair, demanding more. He groans into me, devouring my mouth harder now, our kisses becoming more urgent, blocking out everything except our overwhelming need for each other.

Finally, he pulls away and rests his forehead against mine. "I wish I could stay, but I need to get to the yard, and you should probably go back to bed and sleep off your hangover. We'll celebrate tonight when you're feeling better, but you should know I'm going to take you up on your suggestion from last night."

Heat crawls up my neck, as I remember the way I'd brazenly asked him to take me to bed. Matt stands and lowers his lips onto the top of my head and gently kisses my hair. "Sleep your hangover away, gorgeous, and I'll see you later."

Love fills my heart as I gaze up at him, and I know with absolute certainty that I've found the love of my life, and I'll always belong to this beautiful man. I send a silent message of thanks to Sara who, somehow, had helped Matt to find the peace he so desperately needed so he could let go of the past and begin living again. Perhaps Sara was making right the wrongs of the past for both of them.

And did Rich have a part to play in bringing us together, too? On that awful day when he'd died, so many years ago now, I'd known he'd find some way to love and protect me as he always had, because why would it be any different in death?

Whatever the truth, we're finally together, and the future is ours.

Chapter 53 – Matt

Like a fish gasping for air after being caught on a hook…

I watch from my upstairs office window as Belle parks her car and walks into the centre with her usual self-assurance. Her appearance is as immaculate as ever. She's wearing tailored black trousers and a cream silk blouse which looks both stylish and expensive, but I notice, rather than her signature heels, she has on flat black patent pumps. I wonder why she's insisted on coming in person when we could have organised a change of livery yard over the phone. But I quickly dismiss the thought as I walk downstairs to greet her and we kiss each other amicably on the cheek.

"Let's have some coffee and then you can tell me what brings you here." I suggest.

Belle takes a seat and I sink down in the chair next to hers rather than behind my desk. From my seat, I study her more closely and notice how tired she looks. Her usual pale skin seems even paler today and her emerald eyes stand out like intense green pools. Her nails, which are always perfectly manicured and varnished, are bare of polish and she's picking at her thumb nail absently as she looks across at me. Something's clearly bothering her and I can't help asking.

"Are you okay?"

Tears well up in her eyes, and she swallows as if bracing herself for what she's about to say. As I wait for her to speak, a sense of uneasiness creeps over me, and when she finally frees her words, my entire world is shaken to its core.

"Are you absolutely sure?" I ask, hoping against hope it isn't true.

"Yes, there's no doubt." And with that phrase, my life irrevocably changes forever.

***

After Belle's gone, I sit at my desk, listening to the sound of my heartbeat thumping against my chest, and contemplate her words. One word, actually. *PREGNANT!* Belle is pregnant with my baby.

I replay our conversation over in my head and try to think what the hell I'm going to do.

"Are you absolutely sure?"

"Yes, there's no doubt."

"How? I mean, of course, I know how, but we've always been so careful."

"You of all people should know that protection isn't foolproof, Matt. Look, I know it's a shock. It was a shock for me too. But now I've had a bit of time to get used to the idea, I'm excited about it and I'm sure you will be too once you've thought about it. You've always wanted Tobias to have a

brother or sister - to be part of a family. I want that too - you, me, Tobias, and our baby. I want that more than anything."

I'd hardly taken in what Belle was saying. My mouth was dry; my emotions spiralling out of control. Everything she said was true. I'd always wanted Toby to have a sibling and to be part of a happy family, but this wasn't the way I'd imagined it at all.

"How many weeks are you?"
"About 14 weeks, I think."
"How are you feeling? Are you doing okay – you know, with morning sickness and stuff?"
"I feel a bit rough in the mornings, but it's getting better."
"So, have you had your first scan? Is everything okay with the baby?"
"I'm booked in the day after tomorrow, actually."
"Can I come with you?"
"There's really no need, Matt."
"Please, Belle, I'd really like to."

We'd talked some more. Actually, Belle had talked, and I'd listened in a daze, my mouth gaping open like a fish gasping for air after being caught on a hook. Then, after she'd left, her announcement repeated on a loop, over and over in my head, until I couldn't stand it any longer.

***

"So what's up?" Harry looks questioningly at me as we take our seats in a quiet corner of the pub, where I hope we won't be overheard. "It's not like you to bunk off work for a sly pint."

It's not beer I need, I think ruefully. More like the same quantity of whiskey that Rosie had put away last night. But the truth is that won't change anything, so I'd be better off sticking to a beer and a clear head.

"How's Rosie's hangover?" Harry grins. "I gather from Caz she was pretty upset with you. Have you two made up yet?"

Misery pummels my stomach, as I think back to earlier this morning. I'd finally admitted to Rosie that I wanted a committed relationship with her, but now, with Belle's shock revelation, would that still be possible? And then my misery mixes with guilt, because I realise how devastated Rosie will be when I tell her the news of Belle's pregnancy.

I'm aware that Harry's studying me, waiting for me to speak. I need to say something, but the words are stuck in my throat. "Are you okay, mate?" Harry's tone has changed to concern, so finally, my heart racing, I exhale and tell him.

"Belle wants to keep the baby and for us to make a go of it as a family." I finally trail off, my chest compressing with despondency so I can hardly breathe.

"What are you going to do?" Harry drains his beer, and I see shock and compassion in his face.

"Man the hell up, I guess." I squeeze my eyes shut, as another wave of gut-wrenching pain kicks me in the stomach.

Chapter 54 – Matt

I can't lose Rosie.

Thunder's powerful muscles pulsate beneath me as he obeys my commands with complete trust and respect. We gallop through open fields, feeling the rush of air as we increase speed, riding harder and faster, and gradually the tightly coiled tension eases from my body. We're almost flying, eating up the distance, both of us relishing the adrenaline thrill. And when I finally bring Thunder to a halt, I know he's as exhilarated as I am from the intensity of our wild ride.

I dismount and gaze down at the view of the pretty Cotswold villages scattered in the distance. I'm at the top of the hill at the exact spot where I'd taken Rosie riding, and I'd told her about Sara. Memories of the past, like a blurry watercolour, drift into my mind, and I let the hazy images slowly unfurl and come to life.

My last year at university…I'd spent all my days and nights with Sara. We'd become inseparable, both bright enough to pass our exams without too much effort, so we'd thrown ourselves into the usual student hedonistic lifestyle — drunken parties, sex and sleeping. When the year was over, we should have realised that our relationship had run its course, but instead we'd gone travelling. Then, after Sara's pregnancy, everything had slowly unravelled.

I'd done my best to love her; to be the husband she'd wanted. But, in truth, we'd got married because of her pregnancy, and we'd both tried to make the best of it. We weren't a match made in heaven – far from it - our relationship was often strained and difficult. Forced to be together for the sake of a baby brought neither of us any happiness. Perhaps that was why it was so hard to forgive myself when Sara died, because I felt I hadn't loved her enough or been the husband she'd deserved.

For years I'd put up hard concrete walls to protect my heart from falling in love again. And I'd succeeded. I'd only ever had one-night stands or casual flings, which satisfied my lust but did nothing for my fragile heart. But then, slowly Rosie had made me realise I could finally let go of the past and trust again. She'd healed my broken heart and I know, without a shred of doubt, that I'm in love with her, and I want us to spend the rest of our lives building a future together.

But now Belle had dropped the bombshell about her pregnancy and that she wanted us to be together – to be a family. I remember the guilt I'd felt at being unable to save my marriage to Sara. I'd failed to keep my family together then – wouldn't I be doing the same thing now if I turn Belle down?

And no matter how much I love Rosie, if we're together, I'll have to accept being a weekend father and maybe watch my child being brought up by another man when Belle inevitably meets someone else. Would I be able to do that or would bitterness and resentment creep in, making me regret my decision?

I can't lose Rosie. The words reverberate like an echo over and over in my mind. *I can't lose Rosie.* I sit thinking, hopelessness filling my head, as I try to work out what the hell I'm going to do.

Chapter 55 - Rosie

I'm sorry I'm the one to tell you…

WhatsApp:
Matt: Hi. Hope you're feeling less hungover?
Matt: Something's come up, so I'm going to be late. Sorry.
Me: I'm feeling more human, thanks. No prob. Toby and I will eat, and I'll save food for when you get home.
Matt: Great. Thanks.
Me: Is everything okay?

I can see the dots as Matt types, but then they stop. Watching the screen intently, I wait, but he doesn't reply.

***

By the time I collect Toby from school, I've slept off my hangover and I'm bouncy with happiness. I haven't heard from Matt since his message earlier, but, as he's going to be late, there's no need to rush home. On the spur of the moment, I decide to call in to see Caz and share the amazing news that Matt and I are finally together.

"I'm so sorry for my behaviour last night." I hand Caz a bouquet of scented yellow roses and freesias I've bought from the florist in the village, with an apologetic smile.

"You really didn't need to, but they're beautiful." Caz nuzzles her nose into the colourful blooms and takes a long sniff of their heady aroma. "Come in and have a cuppa. I've got some chocolate birthday cake, Toby, if you'd like some?"

"Yeees pleease." Toby rushes past me into the house before I can stop him, and we both follow, laughing. Once he's happily occupied with a large slice of cake and watching a cartoon on Caz's iPad, I tell her about Matt and me.

"I'm so pleased for you both." Caz beams from ear to ear as she pulls me in for an enormous hug. "Harry and I hoped Matt would finally get his act together. Anyone can see you're right for one another." She pauses. "What's the situation with Belle, though?"

"Matt's meeting her to arrange a change of livery for her horse. I was completely wrong about them getting back together." Relief shows on my face as I smile back at her.

"Well, thank goodness he's finally had some sense and blown her into touch."

"I'm just so happy and…" I trail off as Caz's phone pings, and she drops her eyes to the incoming message. I watch as her smile rapidly fades, replaced by an expression I can't quite read - astonishment or shock, maybe?

"Is everything okay?" I ask quietly, though I know it can't be because her face has drained of colour, and when she looks at me, there are tears pooling in her eyes.

"Caz?" I repeat more urgently. "What's the matter? Is it Harry? Is Harry okay?"

Finally, Caz clears her throat and looks at me. "Sorry – umm – Harry's fine. I – umm – I think you need to talk to Matt."

"Why? What do you mean? Why do I need to talk to Matt?" Alarm races through me as I remember his text message from earlier, when he'd told me something had come up. "Caz, whatever it is, I need you to tell me NOW!" I plead. Something's clearly wrong, and I'm trying hard not to raise my voice, so I don't alarm Toby, but if it involves Matt, then I need to know.

Caz looks at me and I can see she's torn, indecision written all over her face. "CAZ," I say again firmly and eventually she leans over and takes hold of my hand.

"I'm sorry that I'm the one to tell you." She pauses and swallows down hard. "I'm so sorry, but Belle's pregnant."

***

"Wait – what?" I shake my head, not comprehending what Caz is saying.

"I'm so sorry." Caz squeezes my hand. "Matt told Harry at lunchtime."

I gape at her, slowly trying to grasp her words. "Belle's pregnant? No – that's not true," I say firmly because I refuse to believe it.

"I'm so sorry," Caz repeats while I continue to shake my head in disbelief. "Matt told Harry at the pub at lunchtime, and then, when they got back to the yard, Matt took Thunder out. He's been gone all afternoon and Harry's worried about him because he's still not back." Caz stops talking and bites down on her bottom lip.

"No, there's been a mistake," I murmur miserably and my heartbeat thunders against my rib cage as I try to absorb her words.

Just then, another message pings on Caz's phone. "Matt's just got back, and Harry's going to check he's okay."

"I need to take Toby home."

Caz nods and all I see is compassion in her kind eyes. "Are you going to be alright?"

"Yeah, of course." I lie, because my happiness, like the fleeting warmth of summer, has disappeared.

***

Finally, I've persuaded Toby to go to bed. He'd been determined to wait up for 'dad to get home' but it's now 8 o'clock and he's unable to fight his tiredness any longer. His dark expressive eyes, the same shade as his father's, flutter closed as I lay his Thomas the Tank Engine duvet over him and kiss him softly goodnight. I gently brush his fringe away from his eyes – *he needs a trim* - and I sit next to his bed, watching as his breathing becomes more rhythmic and slumber finally takes him.

My heart's so full of love for this little 6-year-old boy who, for the briefest time, I'd dared to dream would become my family. Aching loneliness engulfs me as I realise that won't happen now. I sit surrounded by Thomas the Tank trains and colourful bits of Lego left scattered on his bedroom floor and silent tears glide slowly down my cheeks at the heart-breaking decision I've been forced to make.

Chapter 56 – Matt

Don't hey me…

I've spent hours thinking, trying to get my head around my shock at Belle's pregnancy and what the hell I'm going to do. It feels like I'm in the eye of a raging storm, the brutal elements battering my soul, as I think of a future without Rosie. Somehow, little by little, she's made me laugh again; to feel again. She's pure and good and, without me even realising, she's banished my demons and made me whole again. I love her, and that simple truth calms my inner turmoil, because there is only one certainty. Whatever the compromises I must make, whatever the future is, I want Rosie by my side. Actually, it's more than want; it's vital, like having air to breathe.

I'm finally contemplating heading home when Harry messages apologising, because Caz has broken the news of Belle's pregnancy to Rosie. Fuck*!* I should have had the guts to tell her earlier. Only the coward in me had stopped me, and now it's too late. While I'd been indulging in my own private pity party, Rosie's been dealing with the news alone.

***

It's nearly 9 p.m. by the time I walk wearily into the house. It's ominously quiet. Toby's probably asleep as it's long past his bedtime, and there's no sign of Rosie either as I make my way upstairs to her room.

I take a deep breath and knock softly. "Rosie? Can I come in, please?" There's no reply. "Rosie?" I say more loudly, but there's still no answer, although I can hear muffled sounds coming from within. "Please, Rosie. I know you're in there. We need to talk."

"Go away," she instructs, followed by a strangled sob.

"I'm not going anywhere until we've talked," I say more firmly.

There's an excruciatingly long silence, and I'm contemplating begging, if need be, when she finally opens her door. It's obvious she's been crying, and it tears me apart to know I'm the cause of all her pain. She quickly turns away and walks over to the window, gazing outside as if maybe she can't bear to look at me.

"Hey–,"

"Don't hey me!" She spits out.

I inhale a deep breath, but before I can say anything, she snaps, "I know Belle's pregnant. Caz didn't want to tell me, but I was there when Harry messaged, so I made her. Anyway, I suppose it's saved you the job of telling me." She stops talking and, even though I can't see her face, I know she's crying again.

"I'm so sorry." I walk slowly towards her and try to put my arms around her. More than anything, I want to reassure her that everything's going to be all right.

"Don't touch me," she hisses.

My arms drop back down to my sides in dismay. "Rosie, please, I know this is a terrible shock, but we'll work it out, I promise."

"No...no, we won't. Your future is with Belle now, and you'll finally have the family you've always wanted. I've rung the agency and they say, if you email them my reference tomorrow, they'll put me forward for a couple of jobs they have on their books."

My heart's hammering against my chest, and I can't believe what I'm hearing. Her words are like bullets piercing my body. "I can't lose you," I cry out, my voice racked with unbearable pain.

"I was never yours to lose, Matt." Her voice has finally lost its anger and is deathly quiet. She slowly turns around and her eyes, the colour of sea glass, look at me with such sadness I reach out again to take her in my arms and this time she lets me. We stand together in the fading light, clinging onto each other like we're on a broken raft at sea that's slowly sinking into a deep abyss.

Finally, I gently pull away so I can see her face. My next words are probably the most important ones I'll ever say. I'm taking a chance, but if I'm right, then... "Please hold off the job applications for a couple of days."

"Why, what's the point? You know I can't stay."

"I get that. I really do, but just give me 48 hours. It's the Summer Charity Ball in two days and you can't miss that."

It's a lame reason, but I really hope the pleading look I'm giving her will convince her.

Rosie's expression is confused, but I don't elaborate further. Then she heaves out a sigh. "Okay, two days and then you'll send the reference?"

"I promise. In fact, I'll hand deliver the bloody thing if necessary." I try to lighten the moment, but my voice cracks with emotion.

"Two days." Rosie nods and I hope with all my heart that my gamble will prove right.

Chapter 57 - Rosie

Why Couldn't It Be Me?

I almost hate Matt.

When he'd walked into my room earlier, I'd wanted to lash out - to hurt him as much as he'd hurt me – burning jealousy fuelling my anger at the news that Belle's pregnant with his baby.

Why Couldn't It Be Me?

Then I saw his distraught face, and my anger had instantly burnt itself out. Only sadness remained in the dying embers; the ashes of a future we might once have shared.

Once Matt's found a replacement nanny, I'll have to explain to Toby why I'm leaving; to find the right words to say goodbye to the little boy asleep in the room along from mine.

A little boy I've grown to love.

A lightning bolt of bitterness relights my anger, and I'm back to hating Matt again...*almost.*

Chapter 58 – Matt

A lot rides on the next 48 hours…

It's nearly midnight and I'm sitting alone at the kitchen table sipping whiskey, the amber liquid softening the hard edges of this wretched day. I feel exhausted yet, weirdly, wide awake, adrenaline racing through my body as I play over my earlier exchange with Belle when she'd blown my world apart with her pregnancy news. Rosie's made it crystal clear that whatever future we might have had together is no longer possible. She's walking away and, to be honest, I don't blame her. I'm shredded with sadness at losing her, yet powerless to do anything about it. However, she's agreed to my request to hold off submitting her reference for 48 hours, but I can tell she thinks I'm procrastinating, which, of course, I am.

Outside, the heavy darkness matches my sombre mood. I can hear the screech of a barn owl nestling nearby, which briefly distracts me from my introspection. I need to get my head together because in two days' time, the annual Summer

Ball, the biggest social occasion in the community calendar, will take place at the centre. Each summer we raise much needed funds for various worthwhile local charities that rely on our support and each year we do our best to surpass last year's total. All tickets were sold-out months ago and local companies and benefactors have generously donated gifts for an auction, which will be the climax of the evening.

My secretary, Hannah, who runs the office at the centre, has been organising the event for months. Tomorrow a marquee will be erected, with a bar, dancefloor, 'starlight' ceiling, chandelier, tables, chairs and floodlights. A firm of caterers and waiting staff have also been hired and Caz will perform, supported by a local band, with a variety of music styles to suit all tastes. Like a well-oiled machine, the arrangements are now in place to make the evening a roaring success.

I knock back the rest of my drink while contemplating the next 48 hours: Belle's hospital scan, the Charity Ball, Rosie's reference; a lot rides on the next 48 hours.

Chapter 59 – Rosie

A problem shared is a problem halved...

I'd wanted to avoid Matt at breakfast but, by the time Toby and I come downstairs, he's made a stack of blueberry pancakes, so I can't escape. We sit around the kitchen table eating – Matt chatting companionably to Toby – me, trying my best to ignore Matt's obnoxiously good mood. Why is he so cheerful?

Perhaps he's relieved the decision is made. I'll be leaving shortly, and he and Belle will have a new baby. Every so often, I throw a dagger glare his way, hating his nonchalant attitude, but he seems oblivious. A bitter taste hits the back of my throat, reminding me of the unpleasant coffee Matt used to make me, and waves of nausea roll around my stomach.

I'd drink coffee for the rest of my life, if only Belle wasn't pregnant.

I put down my fork, pushing the pancake to the side of my plate, my appetite gone. *Does that man even have a heart!* Only 24 hours ago, he'd told me he loved me; we were planning our future together. Now his words feel empty and meaningless.

It's my fault. Last night I'd told him we were over, and he's only respecting my wishes, but still…

He's moving on, and I know I need to move on too… *but how can I when he's the only man I'll ever want?*

***

There's a tangible buzz of excitement and anticipation, and only one topic of conversation at the school gate, when I drop Toby off at school. The Summer Ball's tomorrow night and a small gathering of mums are chatting animatedly about who's got tickets and, importantly, what everyone's wearing. I feel a bit like Cinderella because I haven't got a ticket and, even if I had, I can't bear the thought of watching Matt and Belle share their baby news with everyone.

"Fancy a cuppa at the cafe?" I hear Caz calling out, and she's with Janine too, as they both walk towards me waving.

"Yeah, that'll be great," I reply, waving back. I'll literally be waving them a permanent goodbye soon, I reflect, as they both hurry over. Clearly, Caz has broken the news of Belle's pregnancy to Janine, as she embraces me in a hearty sympathetic hug. Tears sting the back of my eyes and I swallow them down hard. *I will not cry… I will not cry… I repeat over and over to myself.*

***

Like the softest cashmere blanket, my totally awesome girlfriends wrap their gentle love around me as I gulp out painful sobs in a quiet corner of the café garden, away from prying eyes.

"So let me get this straight. Matt wants you at the Charity Ball, after which he'll send in your reference?" Caz presses her lips together in a tight line of disapproval, while Janine hands me a tissue to wipe my eyes.

"Yes." I sniff. "Though I don't have a ticket or anything to wear – and even if I did, I don't think I could handle seeing Matt there with Belle."

"Well, the ticket isn't a problem. All Matt's employees are invited, so that would include you. As for a nice dress, we've got all day to find you one. How about we head into Cheltenham and have a girlie day out?"

Janine squeezes my hand. "I think that's an excellent idea. Liam's asked me to go with him and I haven't got anything to wear either, though I don't have a lot of spare money so it might have to be something from a charity shop."

"That's sorted then. Let's drink our tea and head off." Caz smiles at me but then quirks a questioning eyebrow as she notices my hesitancy.

"It's very kind of you both, but I'll feel really awkward if I go…" I trail off.

"Of course, you should go. It's Matt that should feel awkward, not you. And why should you stay away when it'll be a great night? Not to mention, I'll be singing so…" They both look at me pleadingly.

"Okay." I nod in surrender, giving them a watery smile. "Let's do this."

***

The expression 'shop till you drop' probably explains why my poor feet are aching so much. I sit in one of the comfortable wingback chairs in the kitchen, massaging one after the other. We've been to every charity and clothes shop that Cheltenham has, trying on what seems like hundreds of garments under Caz's critical scrutiny. Thankfully, both Janine and I have found reasonably priced dresses for tomorrow night's event, though I'm still unsure if I'll have the courage to go.

Mrs B is here. It's not her usual day, but she's helping to set everything up in the marquee tomorrow, so she's come in for a few hours. I'm grateful to see her, especially as she's taken Toby upstairs to 'help' her. I'm weary from the shopping trip, but it's not just that. There's dejection and hurt at Matt's behaviour at breakfast this morning too. He'd acted as if nothing had changed between us, whereas everything has.

"Here, I've made you a nice cuppa. You poor love, you look done-in."

I'm aware of Mrs B's kindly voice as I drag myself away from my brooding thoughts, and she hands me a mug of strong builder's tea. "Thank you." I smile at her gratefully. "I suppose I should start on Toby's tea."

"Now don't you be worrying about him. I've given him a drink and a biscuit, and he's busy upstairs pairing his dad's socks. Then I've asked him to tidy away his Lego and if he does it properly, I've said I'll give him another biscuit."

"Bribery, Mrs B?" Matt's deep voice resonates around the kitchen as he walks in, smiling.

"Bribery, it may be, but this young lady needs a rest. And it won't hurt to give the young lad a biscuit or two. He's a growing boy, and I'm sure it won't spoil his tea."

Matt wraps Mrs B up in a friendly hug and, over the top of her head, looks questioningly at me, probably noticing my glumness. I really can't be bothered to pretend I'm okay when I'm not. Matt may be over his feelings for me, but I can't switch off my feelings for him so easily.

"Why don't you leave us two ladies to have a little natter? Toby's upstairs and I'm sure he's dying to tell you about his day." Mrs B dismisses Matt, and he gives me another curious glance before walking out of the kitchen and upstairs to his son.

"A problem shared is a problem halved." Mrs B sinks down into the other wingback chair and regards me thoughtfully. "I know heartache when I see it, so I'm wondering if it's got anything to do with the fine-looking man upstairs."

I wonder how much she knows, but she doesn't keep me in suspense for very long. "Sometimes problems seem unsurmountable before they get better. Matt's a good man - don't give up on him."

I feel tears pooling in my eyes. She's trying to be kind, but some problems are just too big to solve. "Belle's pregnant!" I gulp out as tears blind me. "Matt and Belle are having a baby," I repeat, in case she needs me to reiterate it.

Mrs B reaches over and grasps my hand in hers. "Like I say, things generally have a way of working out in the end."

I can't see how, I reason to myself, but she's only trying to help, so I nod my head slowly in agreement.

Chapter 60 - Matt

I'm being a jerk...

I've been at the centre since dawn, and it's a buzz of activity and excitement. A bunch of willing volunteers are decorating the marquee with balloons and bunting, and the tables are being dressed. I hear Caz rehearsing in the background and the sound system's being thoroughly checked. There are last minute problems to fix and queries to answer, but the mood inside the marquee is good natured and relaxed.

I'm picking Belle up at 4.00 p.m. for her hospital scan but, until then, I need to focus on overseeing the final details for tonight's big event. The only thing is I can't stop thinking about Rosie. She'd told me last night that she wasn't going to the Charity Ball, but I'd overruled her and insisted she didn't have a choice. Toby's going, at least for the first part of the evening, and, as his nanny, her presence is necessary too. She'd glared at me, but we both knew my employer 'trump-card' outranked her wishes. Then she'd reminded me I 'owed' her a reference before storming off upstairs to bed.

She's mad at me, and there's a good smattering of disappointment in her eyes too. I know she thinks I'm being a jerk and I don't blame her, but I refuse to accept we're over until – well, until I have indisputable proof that we are.

Chapter 61 – Rosie

Stupid Charity Ball…

I'd tried reasoning with Matt; to explain that it would be awkward for me to be at the stupid Charity Ball if he and Belle were there 'together' as a couple. I'd hoped he'd respect my point of view, but he'd told me I needed to be there to look after Toby. He'd delivered the bad news with an ill-disguised smirk, which irritated the hell out of me. Then, when I'd reminded him he needed to submit my reference as agreed, he'd suddenly become distracted by something important on his phone. I'd stomped off to bed, my patience stretched to the limit by this infuriating man.

The next morning, after successfully avoiding Matt at breakfast and dropping Toby at school, I make my way up to the centre.

I can't help a sharp intake of surprise as I step inside the marquee for the first time. An enormous sparkling chandelier hangs down from the middle of the ceiling and there are thousands of fairy lights strewn across the roof, which look like tiny twinkling stars.

Each circular table seats eight and they're already laid with thick white linen cloths and the silverware and wine glasses are gleaming. The colour theme is silver and gold; each table has a small arrangement of white flowers in the centre and there are silver and gold bows on the back of each chair. The overall effect is stunning.

Mrs B has cajoled me into helping to set up the auction so that everyone knows what items they can bid for and a guide starting price. These range from a case of Moet champagne, a weekend at a Michelin-starred Cotswold hotel, two free horse-riding lessons at the centre, a local cheese and wine tasting, a gin making and tasting, an Alpaca experience, a watercolour painting course, a Spa treatment, a hot-air balloon ride, theatre tickets and a meal at a local pub. There are also lots of cheaper ticketed items, so everyone has the chance to bid for something and raise money for worthwhile local causes. There's a large display of photos and information about each item, and everyone can place bids before or during the auction. The highest bid wins.

I watch Matt at a distance throughout the morning, but he doesn't come over to talk to me and I don't seek him out either. I'm still mad at him and the thought of seeing him and Belle together tonight in this magical fairy-tale place fills me in equal measure with sadness and dread.

Chapter 62 - Matt

When were you going to tell me?

Belle and I sit in the busy hospital's reception area, waiting patiently to be called for the ultrasound appointment. The atmosphere between us is tense, because she's tried hard to put me off coming with her, but I've insisted.

"Honestly, Matt, I know you've got a thousand and one things to do before the Charity Ball tonight. It's only the first scan, and there'll be plenty of others for you to come to." Her eyes lock onto mine persuasively.

"I want to be here. Nothing's more important than seeing our baby for the first time." I try to make my smile reassuring, but she's biting down on her bottom lip and appears distracted. She's nervous, I guess, which is completely understandable.

Shifting position on my hard plastic chair, I try to get more comfortable. Belle's sipping water from a bottle as she's been asked by the hospital to arrive with a full bladder, and there are several other women doing the same.

Thankfully, just a few minutes after our appointment time, we're summoned into a small private room and Alex, the sonographer, apologises for having kept us waiting.

"As this is your first ultrasound scan, I'll just run through with you what will happen. Hopefully, today you'll be able to take your first look at your baby, and I'll be able to tell you your due date. I'll also do some measurements to check everything's developing as it should, and I'll check the placenta position too. I'll need to apply slight pressure to your tummy to get a clear view of your baby, so that might be slightly uncomfortable. You're probably a little nervous, but I'm here to answer any questions you have."

Alex has a quiet, competent manner, and I feel reassured she knows what she's doing. After going through a few more formalities, Belle lies down on the bed, and Alex puts a small amount of gel on her tummy and moves a hand-held probe over her skin. Suddenly, a black and white image of the baby appears on the ultrasound screen. We both gasp at the sound of a strong heartbeat, and Alex positions the screen so we can get a better view.

"Well, everything looks fine you'll be pleased to hear." Alex smiles, as I squeeze Belle's hand. "There's a good strong heartbeat, and there's only one baby. From the measurements I've taken, your baby is due on …."

I stop listening. My heart hammers furiously against my ribcage, and I just want to get out of here.

***

There's an uncomfortable silence as we sit in my car in the busy hospital carpark. Outside, people are coming and going, the hustle and bustle in stark contrast to the oppressive stillness between us. I feel my anger building, but I need to hold it in and remain calm. Belle's staring out of the windscreen, her eyes fixed somewhere in the distance.

"When were you going to tell me?" I ask quietly. "Or maybe you weren't ever going to tell me?" I throw out, my voice sounding strained and curt. "Belle!" I say more firmly when she refuses to look at me.

"I don't understand what you mean," she whispers. But she's bluffing. She knows exactly what I mean.

I take a deep, steadying breath and then another one, willing myself to stay in control. "Alex said the baby's 12 weeks. 12 weeks, Belle," I repeat. I wait, the silence in the car accusing and condemning. When she still doesn't say anything, I have no choice but to spell it out to her. "We haven't slept together in, what, over 4 months. When you said you were 14 weeks pregnant, I was prepared to give you the benefit of the doubt, but 12 weeks, Belle…"

"She's wrong, that's all," Belle says softly, but there's no conviction in her voice.

"Tell me the truth," I demand and, when she finally looks at me, tears are streaming down her face.

"I so wanted the baby to be yours. I thought once I had the baby, you'd fall in love with it like you had with Tobias." She's crying harder now, her words coming out in racking sobs.

What the hell! "So, you lied," I rasp out.

"When I found out I was pregnant, I was so scared … I didn't know what to do."

I need to calm her down. Being upset like this won't be good for the baby, but white-hot anger is burning through me. She'd deliberately lied to me and only reluctantly admitted the truth once I'd laid out the evidence that I couldn't be the father. I take a deep breath, trying to calm my emotions.

"Belle, please stop crying. I need you to talk to me. Tell me who the father is?" I wrap my arms around her, pulling her into my chest to comfort her.

She crumples in my arms, her tears wetting my shirt, but then, after a few moments, she pulls away and I hand her a tissue from the glove box to wipe her eyes. Taking a wobbly breath, she finally looks at me with resignation in her eyes.

"Do you remember when we bumped into each other at the Cheltenham Gold Cup? I was there with a group of friends?"

I think back to that day when I'd been at the races with Caz and Harry and I'd collided with Belle, nearly knocking her off her feet. "Yes, I remember."

"Well, a client called Charlie Redworth was there. He's actually a good friend. I did some work for him at his flat in London. Then he asked me to do another commission at his house in Stow. Anyway, I was working late and … well …"

"And – well?" I repeat, because I need her to admit it.

"He's always had a bit of a thing for me and - I don't know - I suppose I was flattered he wanted me, because I knew you were having second thoughts about us; that you were going to finish with me. Anyway, it was late, and he'd cooked me supper, and we'd shared some wine – too much wine – and well – one thing led to another, and we ended up sleeping together. It was a stupid thing to do."

All this time, she'd known I wasn't the father and yet she'd continue to lie to me.

"Does he know about the baby?"

"No," she says so quietly, I can barely hear her.

"You should tell him, Belle."

"Yes, I know, you're right." She nods slightly.

"Do you want me to drive you over so you can talk to him?"

"What, now?" She looks at me, her green eyes wide with alarm.

"Yes, now. There's no time like the present," I say decisively. *I want this over with, but it won't be until Belle finally admits the truth to this Redworth guy.*

I wait for her to argue, but then her shoulders slump in defeat. "What if he doesn't want to know?"

It suddenly occurs to me that maybe he's married, and that's why she was so scared when she found out about her pregnancy. "Is he married, Belle?"

"No... no, he's not married. Well, only to his career like me, I suppose." She smiles ruefully at me, but I'm not going to let her off the hook.

"You've said he's always had a thing for you, so maybe he'll be blown away when you tell him about the baby. Anyway, whatever happens, he has a right to know."

Belle gives me Charlie Redworth's address, and I tap it into the sat nav. As soon as I've dropped her off, I need to talk to Rosie. I just hope I'm not too late.

***

On the drive over to Redworth's house, Belle apologises repeatedly for lying, but I can't bring myself to offer her the forgiveness she wants. I'm still shell-shocked she'd told me such a huge, calculated lie. Worse, if I hadn't challenged her, would she ever have admitted the truth?

I'd asked her why she'd lied, but she'd refused to explain, except to say she'd been scared when she'd found out she was pregnant. I wonder now if it scared her that Redworth would deny paternity, because she had recently come out of a relationship with me, whereas she knew I would never walk away from my responsibilities.

Or maybe she felt I could provide more financial security for the baby than Redworth – though I doubt it was that because, as far as I could tell, he was well-off, and in any case, Belle was making more than a good living from her own business, if she needed to go it alone.

Then another idea occurred to me. I'd hurt Belle when I'd broken up with her, so maybe lying about paternity was her revenge. She can certainly be headstrong and spoilt at times, and she'd been spiteful towards Rosie on more than one occasion. But could she be that vindictive?

Another explanation was that she'd contrived this whole lie because she was in love with me and wanted us to stay together, no matter what. But that didn't make sense either. Belle knew that Sara and I had rushed into a marriage because of an unplanned pregnancy, and it had been an unmitigated disaster. Why the hell would she think, by repeating history, we'd be any different? Surely, she wasn't arrogant enough to think it was worth the risk?

The only other reason I could think of was panic on Belle's part once she'd discovered she was pregnant, and that seemed the most plausible explanation. She'd admitted to being scared, so maybe it was that simple. She knows how important I think family is and how much I love Toby and want a sibling for him one day. Did she lie to me, because it was easier than facing the truth and the possibility of rejection by Redworth and having to raise the baby alone?

Bitterness crawls up my throat as I realise that, whatever the explanation, she'd been prepared to casually throw away my future happiness for her own selfish reasons. For that, and for losing Rosie, I couldn't forgive her.

Rosie... I'd been unhappy for so long, but then she'd breezed in, the day she'd arrived late for her interview, and changed my life. She'd been the single point of brightness in my prison of darkness and had smashed down the concrete walls that had imprisoned my heart. But what if I've lost her because of Belle's outrageous lie?

Belle exits the car, and I watch as she walks up to Charlie Redworth's town house. I've promised to wait a few minutes in case he's not alone and she needs to make her escape. While I'm killing time, I try calling Rosie, but her phone's switched off, or maybe she knows it's me and doesn't want to take the call.

I make several more attempts and finally leave her a message to ring me back. Then I phone Mrs B to ask her a favour and Harry to warn him I'm running late and to give him the good news. My body's wired with adrenaline and relief that I'm not the father of Belle's baby, but that's old news now. What's important is that I get home as quickly as possible and make things right with Rosie.

Chapter 63 – Rosie

Sorry – what? Say that again…

Matt's been ringing me every few minutes, but I refuse to pick up. I glare at my phone as it loudly vibrates again, and then he leaves yet another message imploring me to ring him back. Well, too bad, because there's no way I'm doing that. A pang of guilt pricks at my conscience, as I wonder why he's phoning so persistently, but an even more stubborn part of me refuses to care. I'm still his employee for now, but as long as I'm fulfilling my professional nanny duties with Toby, I'm determined to have as little contact with Matt as I can.

I've collected Toby from school, and we're both eating our way through a mountain of ice-cream and chocolate while sitting in the garden. It's my petty rebellion against Matt, who prefers him to have healthy snacks, as I usually do. But today is an 'exception to the rule' type of day, especially if I'm to survive the next few painful hours.

"That's probably enough ice cream for now." I cajole. "We'll be eating later with daddy, so you don't want to be too full. How about you have a nice cooling shower, and then you can watch some cartoons before it's time to go out to dinner?"

As Toby sneaks another chocolate flake into his triple scoop of strawberry ice-cream, an uncomfortable thought dawns on me. Stuffing Toby full of too much sugar just before a big formal event, when he's expected to behave impeccably, isn't one of my best ideas. I sigh resignedly and think about the long, awkward evening ahead.

A green-eyed monster thought suddenly pops into my mind as I imagine Matt and Belle announcing their baby news to the guests later. I hastily grab my own chocolate flake and wolf it down greedily. Too much sugar for both of us – way to go Rosie!

***

Caz is shouting down the phone at me, "Rosie, Matt's just told Harry he's not the father of Belle's baby."

"Sorry, what? Say that again," I instruct because I can't take in what she's saying.

"Matt's been trying to get hold of you to tell you. He's NOT the father of Belle's baby," Caz yells as if I'm hard of hearing.

I stare at the phone, trying to make sense of her words, but my brain isn't working properly.

"Rosie, are you still there?" She sounds worried, and I realise she's waiting for me to say something.

"Yes…yes I'm still here."

"Did you hear what I said?" She says more quietly. "Matt-Isn't-The-Father." She emphasises each word like she's talking to a child.

"Matt isn't the father," I repeat back at her, and I feel tears streaming down my face.

"No, he's not. He's been trying to phone you, so you need to ring him back." Caz is laughing hysterically now, and I'm laughing right back at her and crying all at the same time.

After I end the call, I try ringing Matt but, frustratingly, he's not picking up. The irony of the situation isn't lost on me. He'd tried ringing me many times earlier, obviously to tell me the news, but I'd defiantly ignored his calls. Now the cruel gods are taking their revenge.

Time ticks sluggishly by as I wait for Matt to get home. I help Toby get ready and I do the same. Then we sit at the kitchen table, and I find a cartoon for Toby to watch to pass the time, but I'm too distracted to pay attention. Nervous apprehension twists my stomach. Matt had told me he loved me, but what if he's changed his mind?

A childhood memory floats into my mind that if you blow all the seeds off a dandelion with a single breath, then the person you love will love you back. It feels like my future hangs on the breath of fate, as I anxiously wait to find out if Matt still feels the same way about me as he did before Belle hurled a wrecking ball at our lives.

Finally, a few minutes before 7pm, Matt walks into the kitchen. There are dark shadows under his eyes and furrowed worry lines on his face. He looks wrung out with tiredness, but when his deep brown eyes lock onto mine, I lose myself in them. I love him so much. Please let him love me back.

Chapter 64 – Matt

There's so much I want to say…

My tyres crunch loudly on the gravel driveway and shards of stone flick in all directions as I swerve my car to a halt outside the house. I've broken a fair few speed limits in my haste to get home, but I don't care.

At this moment, Belle's undoubtedly telling Charlie Redworth of his impending fatherhood, but, as I walk into the kitchen, my thoughts are elsewhere. My heart's strumming fast against my chest, uncertain of the reception I'm going to receive. Rosie's deservedly mad at me, and it's up to me to make things right and if that involves a grovelling apology and begging, then so be it.

Rosie and Toby are sitting together at the kitchen table and when they notice me, they both look up. From the sounds of it, they're watching a cartoon on Rosie's iPad and Toby absentmindedly murmurs, "Hi dad," before dropping his eyes back down again to focus on the screen.

My throat's dry, and I swallow. "Rosie," but she's already making her way purposefully towards me with a wide smile on her beautiful face. She stands on tiptoes and wanders her fingers up my chest and around the back of my neck. I'm confused, unsure what's going on, but I like this welcome. I like it a lot.

"It's okay. I know." Her voice is warm and calming, soothing away all my uncertainties, and making my heartbeat return to its regular rhythm.

"Yeah?" My voice comes out gravelly and deep.

"Yeah, Caz told me."

"Caz?" I can't help groaning. "We really need to stop communicating through her." I laugh wryly while wrapping my arms tightly around her and pulling her into my chest.

After a moment, Rosie murmurs into me, "You knew, didn't you? All that bravado about delaying my reference was because you knew the baby wasn't yours."

I clear my throat and slightly release my grip on her, so I can see her beautiful face. "When Belle first told me it blindsided me, but then the more I thought about it, the more convinced I became. After Sara's unplanned pregnancy, I've always taken protection seriously. Then, when she didn't want me to go with her for the scan, I had a hunch that she'd lied."

Rosie slowly nods and then pushes away from me. "You should get ready – you're going to be terribly late."

My heart drops like a heavy stone - does that mean she's still mad at me? "We need to talk, Rosie. There are things I need to say."

"Okay, but later." Her smile is like sunshine lighting up her face. And that's when I notice she's wearing a stunning off the shoulder aqua-green dress that skims her curves and emphasises her sun kissed skin and the perfect turquoise of her eyes. Her fair hair is twisted up into an elegant chignon which shows off her slender neck and the delicate rose gold earrings she's wearing. She's never looked more beautiful, and it steals my breath away.

There's so much I want to say but, Rosie's right, there isn't time to talk properly now. The Ball is about to begin and there are lots of worthy charities depending on the money we raise at the auction. "Okay, but we'll talk later." I smile back at her and pull her in for one last hug before I finally release her and go upstairs to get ready.

Chapter 65 – Rosie

I hope the more you drink, the larger your auction bids will be!

Even though I'd been inside the marquee earlier this morning, somehow it looks even more magical in the soft evening light. The crystal chandelier sparkles like priceless diamonds and there are masses of people dressed in their best finery; the ladies wearing beautiful dresses and the men in tuxedos or formal dinner suits. Servers are busy handing out glasses of champagne or orange juice together with tiny bite-size canapés.

Until now, I've never seen Matt dressed formally, and his appearance is 'double-take' WOW… in the best, sexiest kind of way. He always looks hot in his everyday attire of shorts or jeans and a faded T-shirt, but tonight he's drop-dead gorgeous in a black tuxedo and crisp white dress shirt. Taking a sideways peek at him, his eyes catch mine and he winks, making a spontaneous giggle leave my lips and sending goosebumps of desire scattering up my bare arms.

Matt holds Toby's hand as we make our way slowly through the throng of people, and every few steps, someone slaps Matt on the shoulder or grasps his free hand to shake. I suddenly spot Janine and Liam standing together. Janine looks beautiful in a red silk dress she'd bought on our shopping trip, and Liam has his arm protectively around her, clearly telling everyone they're together. When we finally reach the front of the marquee, Harry and Caz are waiting for us and I'm drawn into Harry's massive bear hug while Matt does the same with Caz.

"Glad you're here, mate. I was worried I'd have to do the opening speech if you didn't arrive soon." Harry winks at me.

"Yeah, I'm sorry I'm late – it's been one hell of a day." Matt grins. Then he gently squeezes my shoulder before leaving us and making his way onto the stage.

I find Toby's small hand and grasp it in my own as we both listen proudly while Matt welcomes everyone to the event.

"Ladies and Gentlemen, welcome to our annual Charity Ball. We've been holding this event for several years now and it's a great opportunity for us all to get together and support worthwhile charities in our area by having a fun evening and bidding in the auction. We are very grateful to all the local businesses and benefactors who have donated items to the auction so generously. Thank you very much for your support.

"First, though, before we get to the auction, please enjoy dinner and take advantage of the bar, too. I hope the more you drink, the larger your auction bids will be! Remember, this evening is all for charity and your money will make an enormous difference.

"The auction will start at 9 p.m. and you can make your bids at any time until then or during the auction itself, if you prefer. After the auction, there will be live music and dancing to finish what, I'm sure, will be a spectacular evening. Thank you in advance for all the money you raise this evening and have a great night."

The room explodes with rapturous applause as Matt leaves the stage and makes his way over to us. My heart swells with love for this man, but there's nervousness swirling in my stomach, too. Earlier, Matt said we needed to talk, and I wonder if it's about the job reference he'd promised to send once tonight's over. After everything that's happened, I still don't know if he sees our future together or if he's changed his mind. My head spins with endless scenarios and 'what ifs' but there's nothing I can do but wait patiently until Matt's obligations this evening are over.

Chapter 66 – Matt

Nobody does it better…

Finally, the auction is done and, for now, all my responsibilities have been taken care of. I've shaken hands, stroked egos and used my best powers of persuasion to sweet-talk the great and the good into bidding generously at the auction and parting with their hard-earned money. All my efforts have been worth it though because it looks like we've broken last year's record amount by quite a big margin.

Caz is on stage belting out a number, and people are gradually taking to the dance floor. It's the part of the evening I like best because all the formalities are over, and it's time for everyone to relax and have fun. I scan the room looking for Rosie so I can cadge at least one dance with her before someone inevitably pulls me away. She's sitting with Toby and Harry, laughing at something Harry's saying.

"Would you like to dance?" I hold out my hand and Rosie's dazzling blue eyes capture mine before she rises to her feet.

I lead her onto the dance floor just as Caz switches the tempo to a softer, more romantic song. Did Caz do that on purpose or am I just lucky? My arms circle Rosie's waist and she drapes her arms around my neck, while resting her head gently against my shoulder. The mesmerising rhythm of the music flows around us while I hold her close to me, her curves pressing against my body. Slowly, sensuously, her fingers explore the nape of my neck while I lightly rub circles over the small of her back. We sway slightly to the music, oblivious to everything but each other and its perfection.

The song is an old-time classic James Bond theme 'Nobody Does it Better' by Carly Simon, but Caz is singing it in her own unique style, and I never want it to end. I wonder if it'll become 'our song' and we'll both remember this moment when we're old. I pull Rosie even closer, kissing the top of her hair tenderly, but then some idiot taps me on the shoulder. Rosie looks up, startled by the interruption, and the spell breaks. She gives me a quick smile and begins moving away, but I grab hold of her hand firmly. There's no way I'm letting her go.

After a moment, dealing with the guy who disturbed us, it seems everyone's got the same idea because there's a constant stream of people coming up to congratulate me on the success of the evening. I guide Rosie towards the exit of the marquee, but people keep getting in our way, slapping my back or wanting to chat. I'm polite, but I don't stop. I need to get Rosie outside, to be alone with her without all these people milling around us. Eventually, we make it through the crowd, and I lead her off to the side of the marquee and blow out a deep breath.

I've noticed Rosie's eyes change colour depending on her mood. Sometimes, they're the lightest turquoise blue and playful; other times, they're the intense colour of the Mediterranean Sea on a scorching day. I remember when I kissed her; they were dark with desire. They're dark now. The night's full of a thousand glittering stars, and the air's heavy with anticipation between us. It's the perfect moment to kiss her. But then a few people wander out of the marquee and begin heading our way, and I realise I've lost my chance.

"Let's get out of here." I heave out a heavy breath of frustration.

Rosie nods. "I'll fetch Toby."

"No need. He's staying over with Mrs B tonight. I'll just grab his overnight bag from the car."

"Oh? When did you arrange that?" She looks at me in surprise.

I grin back at her. "I phoned her this afternoon, and I packed Toby's overnight bag just before we left."

"That's very devious of you, Mr O'Connell." Rosie raises her eyebrows at me, but from her wide smile, I can tell she's happy.

"Come on, let's say our goodnights and go home."

Chapter 67 – Rosie

All the broken pieces of me…

Thankfully, Matt's brought his car because my 4-inch heels aren't designed even for the shortest of walks. I collapse onto the front seat beside him and begin pulling out the pins securing my hair, letting the unruly waves fall freely over my shoulders.

"You, okay?" Matt looks over at me, smiling.

"I will be when I can kick off these heels and take off my dress." I grin back at him, expecting he'll make a quip about undressing me or another wisecrack, but he remains quiet. My eyes sweep over his face, but his expression is unreadable in the darkness; only the atmosphere feels charged with electricity between us. A tight knot of nervousness twists uneasily in my stomach because I know as soon as we're home, he'll finally tell me how he feels about us and about our future.

A niggling voice of doubt whispers to me. What if he's changed his mind and there isn't any us?

No. I refuse to contemplate that possibility. Because, unless I've completely misread him, when we'd danced together earlier, he'd shown me, with every look and touch, the honesty of his feelings. All the same, worry still stubbornly gnaws at my insides as we drive the short distance home.

Matt stops the car in front of the house and, before I even realise it, he's around to my side, sweeping me up into his strong arms and carrying me over the stony drive.

"Don't want you to ruin your shoes or fall over and break your neck." His voice is low and vibrates against my hair.

Wrapping my arms around his neck, I snuggle into him. I remember the last time he'd carried me was when I'd been drunk, and he'd put me to bed after Harry's birthday. I'm stone-cold sober now and a fluttering of hope caresses me that maybe he'll carry me upstairs again, but this time to his bed and not mine. Hope swaps to disappointment when he carefully sets me down inside the hallway.

The moonlight casts soft shadows as we stand there, neither of us moving or speaking. Then Matt breaks the silence, his words straining against the stillness. "Do you want a nightcap …a whiskey or there's some Champagne in the fridge?"

"No," I murmur, and I take a tentative step closer to him, and then another one, until I'm near enough to feel his laboured breathing. I bring my hand up to his face and gently stroke my index finger along his tight jawline, loving the feel of his rough stubble against my skin as I continue slowly wandering my finger over his cheek.

It's all the invitation Matt needs as his mouth finds mine and his tongue runs along the seam of my lips, demanding entrance. I moan into him as he pushes me back against the hall wall, our bodies coming together, our tongues exploring each other in a voracious dance of desire. Matt's strong arms swoop around me as my legs buckle, and he supports my weight while continuing his rampage of my mouth. He's possessive and alpha and I willingly give myself to him, feeling his hard arousal against me. Fierce heat travels over my body as my fingers fist his shirt and then find their way beneath the material roving over his taut muscles…

"Rosie." Matt's voice is low and gravelly as he gently pulls his mouth from mine. "I'm so fucking sorry for all the pain I've caused you."

"I don't care about any of that," I rasp out. *In fact, all I care about at this precise moment is getting his mouth back on mine.*

Matt nods slowly, his eyes never leaving my face, and he takes my hand, linking our fingers together. "I love you, Rosie. In fact, I think I fell in love with you that first day you came for your interview, and you drew that ridiculous sketch of me on the pantomime horse.

"I'd been so certain I didn't want another relationship after Sara died. I thought I was protecting my heart, but actually, I'd buried it in a deep, dark pit of grief and regret. Even when I began having feelings for you, I kept telling myself it wouldn't work – that I wasn't good enough for you. And, also, you were Toby's nanny, so it felt all kinds of wrong." He grins sheepishly at me. "But then when you told me about your brother dying in Afghanistan, you made me realise how fragile life is and how I needed to make the most of mine.

"After I kissed you that day at the tower, the memories – the pain of losing Sara – everything hurt less, but, being a stubborn arse, I wouldn't allow myself to move on. It wasn't until the night of the salty cupcakes, when I rejected you again, that I finally reached the decision to let go of the past."

Tears are pooling in Matt's dark eyes, and I squeeze his hand gently to let him know I understand about grief, because I do.

"You once asked me if I believed in 'happy ever after' and I said I didn't. But now I know we can be each other's happy ending. You've healed all the broken pieces of me and I want - I need - the joy of loving you."

Swallowing down all the emotions squeezing my throat, I think back to that silly pantomime horse I'd drawn for Toby and how much had happened since then. I'd been grieving too, but we'd helped each other to accept the painful scars from our pasts and begin living again.

"I love you, Matt, so, so much. But I never want you to forget Sara. She'll always be a part of your and Toby's life, just as Rich will always be a part of mine. That'll never change. Grief is part of life, and life is messy and imperfect and complicated. But, as long as we have each other and Toby, we'll deal with it and whatever else may come our way."

I take a shaky breath and Matt nods, gently cupping my cheeks in his large hands. This time his kiss is unhurried and tender, sealing our future with a quiet promise of second chances.

THE END

EPILOGUE

SIX MONTHS LATER - Matt

"Look, dad!" Toby's eyes are bright with excitement as I walk into the kitchen. It's Sunday morning – the best part of the week as far as I'm concerned because there's no school and that means I get to spend all day with Toby and Rosie. The kitchen table is strewn with various crayons and paper, and Toby's pointing his finger at his latest art masterpiece.

I'd left Rosie asleep in our bed and quietly crept out just before dawn to work the early shift at the yard. Despite being the boss, I always take my turn on the rota but, thankfully, the rest of Sunday is free for me to do as I please. Top of my list is making Toby and Rosie's favourite Sunday breakfast – blueberry pancakes with maple syrup.

Rosie's busy brewing her beloved builder's tea and I grab her gently by the waist and lean in to kiss her. Her breath hitches and she shuffles closer, her soft curves fitting perfectly into my body. Her skin is warm and inviting as she presses against me, and I begin slowly tracing small circles against her back. "If Toby wasn't here…." I whisper into her hair, leaving the rest of my words to her imagination.

"Daaad!" Toby impatiently cuts into my indecent thoughts, and I release her with a sigh.

"Okay, let me see, buddy." My pride bubbles up as I look at his picture. It's a waxed crayon drawing of three people and each one is in a different colour and labelled 'Dad,' 'Mum' and 'Toby'. There's also a rather scruffy dog – hmm, no doubt, another attempt to persuade me to give in and allow him a pet.

"That's fantastic, Toby." I stare at the drawing, noticing that Rosie isn't in it. I know I shouldn't be disappointed, but I can't help it.

"It's a picture of our family – me, you and mum." He points to each figure in turn. "And that's Rufus."

"And where's Rosie?" I ask casually, stubbornly ignoring the reference to the dog. That's a discussion for another day. "She's part of our family too, Toby."

"Here!" He looks at me as if I'm being stupid and points at the figure labelled "Mum."

Rosie has moved to stand next to me, and I automatically reach for her hand and link our fingers together while we both stare transfixed at the crayon drawing. "Mum?" I ask carefully, in case I've assumed wrong.

Toby looks up at Rosie shyly. "I want to call you mum. Please, Rosie, can I?"

I wonder what Rosie's thinking and if she's okay with that. We haven't talked about Toby calling her mum, but nothing would make me happier. It would make sense too when we add our baby to the family mix, hopefully in the not-too-distant future. I glance sideways at Rosie and there are tears pooling in her eyes, and I know immediately she's on board with his request.

Even though he's still waiting for an answer, I can't trust myself to speak for a moment. Finally, I clear my throat and squeeze Rosie's hand. "That's a really great idea, son."

Toby beams at us with a broad grin, and then he points to a bright yellow star shining from the middle of a moonlit sky. "And this is my other mum in heaven."

***

ONE YEAR LATER - Rosie

So much has happened... where do I even begin? Well, I guess, first, I should tell you I'm now Mrs O'Connell.

Matt proposed to me in the garden on a beautiful moonlit evening. He'd lit up the patio with hundreds of twinkling fairy lights and candles and, once I'd caught my breath, of course, I said yes. We were married at the small village church less than a month later, with a party afterwards at the centre for all our friends. Harry was Matt's Best Man, and I walked down the aisle with Toby by my side. It had to be Toby because he was the reason I'd come to live here in the first place and why I'd drawn that ridiculous pantomime horse. And Toby was the key to unlocking Matt's happiness.

Matt was a little surprised when I'd suggested taking Toby on our honeymoon to visit his sister and her family in the USA, but, to me, it seemed the perfect thing to do. After all, Toby hadn't met his American cousins, and I couldn't imagine leaving him at home without us. We're a family, after all, and family means everything to both of us.

The honeymoon; spending time with Matt's sister, her husband and children; watching Toby play with his two little cousins – it was amazing – and now they're planning a return visit here next summer.

My second bit of news is that I'm pregnant – a honeymoon baby – which, obviously, we're delighted about; though Rufus is giving the baby stiff competition in the popularity stakes as far as Toby's concerned. And that's my third bit of news. Toby's now the proud owner of a Border Collie puppy, so we'll soon be a family of five. Rufus is the naughtiest, funniest, craziest puppy dog I've ever met, and we all love him to bits… unless he's chewing up shoes left carelessly lying around.

I've also been taking riding lessons at the centre, though that's had to be put on hold for a bit until after the baby comes. Turns out, I'm not bad at riding after all and, more importantly, I really enjoy it. Who knew!

My last piece of news is that I'm studying an accountancy and business qualification at the local adult education centre. The course is part time and fits in with school pickups, and when the baby comes, I'll be able to use their crèche, although Mrs B has already offered to babysit. The plan is I'm going to take on the accounts side of things at the centre, freeing up Matt's time for him to do more of what he loves - working with his beloved horses.

You might also be interested to hear that Janine and Liam have achieved nationally recognised qualifications in English and Maths. They've also just announced their own pregnancy, so our little ones will soon become playmates. And Harry and Caz are on an extended holiday in Australia, so Caz can finally meet Harry's parents. Also, in case you're wondering, Belle married Charlie Redworth in a glitzy high society wedding in London, photographs of which appeared in several celebrity gossip magazines.

Nobody knows what the future holds, but today - this moment - we're living our 'happy ever after'. We're still grieving in our different ways, and we'll always carry the scars from our past, but through acceptance and resilience we're building a future - together.

Our love has healed the broken pieces of us.

Dear Reader

I hope you enjoyed reading The Broken Pieces of Us – Matt and Rosie's story - as much as I've enjoyed writing it. If you did, please leave me a review as they are so important for new authors and help others to discover my book. You can also visit my author's page on Amazon or Facebook. I'd love to hear from you.

Acknowledgments:

During my research for this book, I discovered there were 457 fatalities of UK armed forces personnel during operations in Afghanistan. As Rosie says in the story, they were sons, brothers and husbands and their sacrifice will never be forgotten.

There are over 7 million people described as having 'very poor literacy skills' in England, by the National Literacy Trust. Like Janine in the story, adults with poor literacy skills can find it difficult to get jobs and support their child's learning. If you are one of them, you can seek support from your local adult education centre or college.

There are a few people to thank:

Katie – you've brought my ideas to life with your amazing book cover design.
Barbara - your patience, encouragement and editing skills are so appreciated. Any errors are purely mine.
Sue, Kathryn, Gill, Sarah and Chris – you listened as I endlessly talked about Matt and Rosie and, even after reading the initial drafts, you continued to cheer me on.
Mark and Liya – You encouraged me every step of the way towards my dream to write a book. As Rosie and Matt would say, family means everything, and you do.

Printed in Great Britain
by Amazon